Praise for *The Felsar King*

• • •

"Captivating, intriguing, and ultimately, a story that stays with you long after the last page."
-Kayla Ann, author of *Well of Dreams*

• • •

"This book will captivate you as you journey with Schandrof through times of great faith and trial. Excellent addition to Okoye's world."
-Kaitlyn Deann, author of *The Witches' Sleep*

• • •

"Tranquility and chaos rolled into one poetic fairytale."
-T M Lunn, author of *Skin Deep*

• • •

WORKS BY THIS AUTHOR

The Felsai Morgaron
Goleah's Lore

• • •

Age of the Anathema Series
Tainted
Branded

• • •

Short Stories
The Dead Were Never from Florida
Tales of the Karsha
The Games We Play

The FEISAI MORGARON

XYVAH M. OKOYE

THE FELSAI MORGARON
Published by Two Trees Books
First published worldwide in September 2024.
1st Printing 2024
Edited by Kaitlyn Deann
Text Copyright © Xyvah Okoye, 2024
Map and illustrations by Xyvah Okoye, Copyright © 2024
Character illustrations by Sílvia Gómez
Cover by D. Ellis-Montgomery
The moral rights of the author and illustrator have been asserted.
eBook ISBN: 978-1-915129-61-1
Paperback ISBN: 978-1-915129-62-8,

All rights reserved under international copyright law. No part of this book may be used or reproduced in any manner whatsoever without prior written permission of the publisher, except in the case of brief quotations embodied in critical articles or reviews.

This book is a work of fiction. Names, characters, businesses, organisations, places, events, and incidents are either the product of the author's imagination or are used fictitiously. Any resemblance to actual persons (living or dead), events, or locales is entirely coincidental.

Content warning: mentions/depictions of gore, violence, grief, miscarriage, abuse, disability.

*For all who stand against the darkness.
All who fight for a better world.*

EUTOPIA
AS MAPPED BY
IVANN B. BARTOLOME
PAVOS
WINEHOMEYARD
MURAH
DRAGON'S KEEP
FLOKHAMBE
WATNESBUSE
ROMBERMOUTH
WAFORD
RIVERFORD
GATESBUSE
WODBUTON
CARTON
MAMERS
WIKERUGH
THE GARUA
ROCKERNEWES
Sea of Honley

THE OLD OAK TREE

TOTHAM

BLECLIF

MANOVER

WAGIE

WITBURY

STOTFOD AN

AHWARK

LINVER

KIRTON

PERESEY

LYSTER

CHARY

ALIGHAMBE

MACKINGHAM

TIRE

CATEEORD

BROD

BRAPLE ABIGLE

HESTON

LOGAN

DYPICHEAPLE

MABIGDON

PENZAN

FITONBY

MACKERMING

NOHTON

BRETNESHAM

100 MILES

My dear children,

It has been a time since I have come unto you; and two times since I have given you a commandment to hold fast to, save that of serving the Great Mother with fervour.

Well known to all is the news of Enacia Bluewater's return. That she is well gladdens my heart, though she has returned from the abyss with grave and perilous tidings; for she ventured into the necropolis of the gods and unveiled a hidden text within the catacombs, written in *vientala*[1].

Scribed by the hand of Schandrof himself, this text bears testament to the truths hidden beneath our world—veiled behind layers to deceive the innocent and make monsters of many. It is a book of testimonies[2]: a record of both past and future; history and prophecy; the truth as shown to Schandrof by the goddess, Pyxis, after he first sought her as a child in the Field of Kesindrath.

---

1. The language of the gods

2. *Flesai Morgaron* is the *vientala* translation for *Book of Testimonies*

It details the truth behind the war against Emperor Vladicsar; how Schandrof was chosen by the Warrior God to defeat the Emperor; and also serves as a warning to deter any from straying down the same dark path.

The tale is one I struggle to comprehend, though my soul screams of its authenticity (the matter of the adomin ability to sense the truth is one also detailed within the text, granting it even greater credence).

These are truths which cast our history in a new light and will now reshape the path for our future. I have taken it upon myself to inspect the translation of the script as proposed by the Late Mother Yrnanon, and find it to be accurate. Now, my children, I send a transcript unto you.

Copy it twice, then twice, and thrice more; that even should the original manuscript be lost to time, at least two copies will be held at every temple of the Great Mother (one to be used by the High Priest and the other kept as a reserve).

A new charge has been laid upon my heart.

Gather the wanderers; they must now settle. All among our order must now be bound to a temple. The tenets listed within the text are to be read aloud in the nave of the temple continuously from dawn till dusk, and the entire text read on the feast days of the New Moon, Terigad, Lupa and Yule. Those of the Order of Verit will take turns reading, with one priest starting from the beginning as soon as the other reaches the end.

For this reason, from henceforth, every priest of the Order of Verit shall belong to a group of seven: a Kleris. Each Kleris comprises a High Priest, a novice, a healer, a mage, and three warriors, trained in the martial arts. Every Kleris shall be under the command of its High Priest, and every High Priest shall answer directly to me, the Oracle, who is the spokesperson for the Great Mother herself.

Greis Fionn, Ahren Ardal, Chay Snowfield and Fremont Windsong shall be charged with fulfilling this task. Set scriveners from among you, that they may begin the work of copying. It does not escape me that this charge is great, for you must now provide lodging and upkeep to the wanderers. Break down the temples, if the need arise, and build larger ones that can house every Kleris under its care. Collect an offering from the people to aid in this, for our order has done great good in the east; it is also good that we reap the fruit of our labour.

It is never a mother's wish to impose on her children. I wish only that you thrive as you seek to serve the Great Mother. Soon, I shall come unto you, that your hearts may be comforted and your joy may be complete.

— Mother Sexanon,
The 9th,
Oracle of the Great Mother.

High Priest

Healer　　Mage

Warrior　　Warrior　　Warrior

Novice

THE KLERIS
Priestly Order of Verit

THE TRANSCENSION OF SCHANDROF

The blue melonia have blossomed in the Field of Kesindrath. Their golden pollen floats above the Meadow like a shimmering haze. Might it be a veil between worlds? Might it lead me to Zenthurien; to the realm of the gods; to the place where Pyxis dwells? I shall find out. I shall walk through the field of blue and traverse the fog of gold to find the Great Mother.

My feet feel heavy, and though the air hurts my lungs, I shall sit here among the flowers of the goddess. I shall blow upon their stamens and breathe in the dust of the gods that I might perhaps commune with one.

She came from nowhere. Her feet made no sound upon the field, neither did the train of her flowing white gown whisper as she approached. Her golden hair and bronzed skin shimmered like the cloud of pollen she walked through, and from her head protruded two curled, ivory horns.

I fell on my face in reverence.

She spoke, and her voice was like the sound of a bubbling brook. "Rise, my child," said she.

Climbing to my feet before her, I stared into the face of one who had outlived worlds and outshone a thousand stars. And though I was but a boy, a few moons[1] shy of manhood, my heart was moved by her beauty and grace.

"Three days you have sought me," said she; "three more shall you remain. Three and three things I shall show you: things of the past; things of the present; and the last, pertaining to things which have not yet come to pass."

At her words, I was swept up by a great wind and taken to a field of stars in a deep blue sky, and here, I was shown the things which cannot be unwritten.

---

1. By this time, the measure of time had changed from *years* to *moons,* as the moon was only visible once every five (four and three quarter) seasons, during *Hoadon,* the feast of the gods.

PART ONE
THE PAST WHICH CANNOT BE UNWRITTEN

THE PAST WHICH CANNOT BE UNWRITTEN

Stars danced through the sky, showering beautiful lights over everything. The Great Spirits gathered to watch in awe and wonder as these celestial bodies spun, and dipped, and dived, and swirled; until, finally, they crashed into each other with a resounding clang that echoed like a million struck gongs.

Out of the explosion came realms upon realms, some so great, they rivalled the Great Spirits themselves. These Great Spirits rushed forward, each to claim the realm they would rule over, each being drawn to the worlds most like them. Then fell a great silence and darkness upon everything, and in the peace and quiet of the secret place, Great Spirit Pyxis[1] found Eutopia.

Her realm was a place of magic and mystery; and I beheld vast lands, great hills, and lush meadows. And she ran through the majestic forests with trees so tall that their tops scraped the sky, and she swam in the running streams, so clear that they reflected

---

1. In the original manuscript, the word "she" was used, but scholars later translated this to refer to the goddess, Pyxis, who was not originally counted among the gods and was only deified when Schandrof sought to unite all the religions in his empire under one god.

the stars above. And she loved all the unimaginable creatures in this world, for Eutopia was the most beautiful place in existence.

Thus, she was considered to be the wisest Great Spirit, for Eutopia was a world of wisdom, and she had chosen it.

THE FIRST VISION

One day, as she walked the breadth of her realm, she came upon a river that would not flow. She found it was neglected by fish and people alike. Moved with compassion, she asked the river, "River, why do you not flow?"

To this, the river responded, "My heart is to the east, and my soul is to the west, but I have no body to contain both, so I cannot flow."

Worrisome as the situation was, the goddess was wise as she was compassionate, and although her heart was moved for the river that would not flow, she understood that there is a reason for everything, and an effect to every action. She would not simply create a body for the river that would not flow. Instead, she travelled the lands east of the river in search of anyone who would lend their body to the river that would not flow.

She travelled far and for days, beseeching all she came across to lend their body to the river, but none would listen, and none would help.

After seven suns had risen in the east, she came across a young girl with golden eyes who frowned as she watered her garden.

"Why do you frown as you water your garden?" asked she.

To this, the girl replied, "For weeks and weeks, I have watered my garden, but still the flowers refuse to grow. The seed is good, I know that much. Yet, weeks and weeks have gone by, and still I have no flowers in my garden."

Moved with pity once more, the goddess considered how to help the young girl with golden eyes. She would not simply make the flowers bloom, for she understood that there is a reason for everything, and an effect to every action.

"If the seed is good," said she to the young girl, "then perhaps the soil is unfertile."

"Perhaps," said the young girl. "But I have no other soil, and thus, must use this."

Touched by her plight, the goddess set off north, in search of fertile soil to help the young girl with golden eyes whose flowers refused to grow. For seven suns, she travelled north, beseeching all she came across to give of their soil to the girl with the golden eyes whose flowers refused to grow. Till finally, far to the north, she came across an old man. His braided beard and silver locks trailed down to the soil on which he sat, and his aged eyes searched the skies with worry on his face.

"What do you search for with such worry in your heart?" asked she the man with aged eyes who searched the skies.

To this, the man replied, "I search for rain, for I thirst, and I fear I shall not last beyond a fortnight."

Moved with sorrow for the dying man with aged eyes, the goddess pondered the situation. She would not simply make rain fall, for she understood that there is a reason for everything, and an effect to every action.

Finally, she said, "I shall tell you where to find water, that you might live."

"Tell me," said he, "and I shall heed your words."

"Gather up your soil and head south for seven suns, until you meet a young girl with golden eyes whose flowers do not grow. Thence head west for seven more suns, and you will find a river that does not flow."

Grateful for her instruction, the dying man with aged eyes packed up his soil and headed south. He travelled for seven suns till he came upon a young girl with golden eyes who frowned while she watered her garden.

"Greetings, young girl with golden eyes," said the dying man. "Why do you frown so while you water your garden?"

"Greetings," said the young girl. "For weeks and weeks I have watered my garden, but still, the flowers refuse to grow. The seed is good, I know that much. Yet, weeks and weeks have gone by and, still, I have no flowers in my garden. Perhaps the soil is unfertile, but I have no other soil."

"Then I shall give you fertile soil!" the man exclaimed; "But, in exchange, you will accompany me to the river which does not flow, that I may draw water and live."

Overjoyed, the young girl agreed. She covered her garden with the man's fertile soil and followed him on his journey west.

Seven suns came and went, and the two travellers became fast friends. When they reached the river that the goddess had mentioned to the dying man with aged eyes, the travellers could not draw from it because the river would not flow.

"Why do you not flow for me?" asked the dying man to the river. "Would you have me perish from thirst?"

"Not at all," replied the river. "But my heart is to the east, and my soul is to the west, and seeing as I have no body to contain both, I cannot flow."

Disheartened, the dying man sat on the banks and wept, for it was already fourteen suns and he would perish that day.

The girl watched her friend with tears in her golden eyes, for she had come to care deeply for the dying man with silver braids which kissed the soil. Turning to the river, she asked, "If I offer you my body, will that suffice?"

With a merry heart, the river roared its approval.

"Then I shall give you my body so you may flow and save my friend."

Stepping into the water, the girl with golden eyes was swallowed up within swirling waves, and the river's heart and soul were reconciled, and the river began to flow. It flowed and flowed until the banks overflowed and the dying man drank his fill. As he drank, his youth and vitality were restored, and his aged eyes shone with newness once more.

But his eyes quickly filled with tears, for he realised, in saving him and helping the river, the girl with the golden eyes had given up her own life.

For seven suns, the man and the river mourned the girl with golden eyes who was now gone; and they called the place *Trjindér*, meaning: *place of sorrow*. And after the seventh sun, the man set off home. He travelled east until he reached the garden of the girl, and to his surprise, he found her flowers had all bloomed.

The man was moved to tears, for the girl's golden eyes would never see the beautiful purple flowers in her garden. He wept and wept until his tears washed the flower petals to a pale blue. It was only then that the man heard the voice of the girl with golden eyes whispering to him from the flowers washed with his tears.

"It is well," whispered she. "I am with you. I will always be with you."

Frantic, the man gathered up all the flowers in his arms until the whisper was a steady, solid voice repeating the same words: *It is well. I am with you. I will always be with you.*

Strengthened by her words, the man returned home with the pale blue flowers which promised that the girl with golden eyes would always be with him.

On seeing him arrive with his youth restored and the flowers in his arms, the goddess asked, "How did you fare?"

The man recounted all that had happened, and she listened patiently to all of his words.

"The girl with golden eyes was kind and good to sacrifice so much for you and the river," said the goddess, for she understood that there is a reason for everything, and an effect to every action. "Because of this, though her body remains in the river, her soul will remain in all who drink from it. Her soul, youthful and kind, will always bring healing and health to those nourished by the river that now flows."

"And her heart?" asked the man. "If her body will remain in the river and her soul will remain with all who drink from its waters, what will happen to her heart?"

Taking the pale blue flowers, the goddess buried them in the man's good soil, and from it sprouted an oak tree. The oak tree grew tall and wide, till its branches scraped the sky and its canopy blocked out the sun.

"For her kindness and great sacrifice," said she, "her heart shall be this oak tree, and this oak tree shall endure here to forever watch over this realm."

Falling to his knees, the man wept, for he was mortal and would someday leave his friend's heart, body, and soul behind. "I cannot leave her," begged he. "She saved my life. If she is to remain here, then permit me to remain forever beneath her canopy."

Moved with compassion once more, the goddess obliged, for she understood that there is a reason for everything, and an effect to every action.

Thus, the man with the braided beard and silver locks remained forever with the giant oak tree that was the heart of the girl with golden eyes; for she had given her body that the river may flow and save a dying man; and her soul had restored his youth.

As the great wind returned me to the Field of Kesindrath to lay on the bed of blue melonia flowers, she approached me once more.

"Do you understand the vision?" asked she.

Unable to lie, I replied, "No, I do not."

"The vision is of things which have already come to pass. The vision may be unclear now, but with time, understanding shall come. You need only listen."

I listened, and as I lay among the blue melonia flowers, I heard the faint whisper of a promise: *It is well. I am with you. I will always be with you.* And my heart was comforted by these words.

THE SECOND VISION

Again, I was swept up by another great wind, and I found myself atop the great oak tree that was the heart of the girl with golden eyes who had given her body for the river to flow and whose soul had restored the youth of the man who would never die.

Upon its branches sat the man with long silver locks, but his beard was shaven, and his skin sun-kissed. He stared at me with piercing blue eyes, and I knew it had been a time and times and time again that he had remained upon that tree.

And upon the land, the people had increased and multiplied and become a great many in number. And from among them were chosen a score and one; and to them was given great might, that they may lead the people.

The man upon the tree turned his face to the south, and I saw a great wave come up from the sea. And the waters of the sea covered the land and swallowed up a third of it. And I saw the people of the land swallowed up, along with their possessions and livestock. But the sea was not a cruel soul, and so it granted the people the ability to live beneath its surface. And thus, a third of the people descended to live beneath the waves.

And the man called the sea *Honohley*[1], which means *Here, we are welcome*; for it had taken a third of the earth and given them a home beneath its waves.

Then the man turned his face to the west, and I saw a great wind descend from the sky. And the wind swept across the land and swallowed up a third of it. And I saw that the people of the land too were swallowed up, along with their possessions and their livestock. But the wind, like the sea, was not a harsh soul, and it granted the people the ability to fly. And thus, a third of the earth ascended to live among the heavens.

And the man called the wind *Oragon*, meaning *The one who lifts us up*; for it was sent by the Winged One[2], and it had taken a third of the people and given them a home among the stars.

Finally, the man turned his face to the east, and I saw that only a third of the people remained.

Then spake I to the man with sun-kissed skin and silver locks and piercing blue eyes, "What does this mean?"

To this, the man replied, "It has been but a time and times and time again I have watched the lands change. The people are no longer kind like the girl with golden eyes who gave her body to the river that would not flow."

---

1. In time it has come to be known as the Sea of Honley, situated south of the continent, beyond the border widely referred to as *Siren's Bay*. The border derived its name due to the myth that the Sea of Honley was (and still is) ruled by Moreto, the Siren Prince.

2. In reference to the Ancient One sometimes referred to as *the Watcher* or *the Master*. It is believed that he is one of the three Sons of Skalas, among the first fruits of the Creator, the Prince of Darkness who was once the Prince of Light.

I perceived he spoke such words because he understood not that the people of the lands had never been kind, and he knew not that the goddess had besought many to help the river that would not flow and the girl with golden eyes whose flowers did not grow. Then asked I the man with sun-kissed skin and greying locks and piercing blue eyes: "But if the sea is not cruel and the wind is not harsh to the people who are not kind, then what is the meaning of the vision? For the people are unkind, and this way they have always been."

"I see all," said the man, "yet blind am I to the ways of this world. I am wisdom and foolishness, hope and despair, suffering and relief. I am aged, yet ageless, existing, yet removed from the annals of life. I am nameless, timeless, faceless. And though I am blind to the ways of this world, I see all."

As the great wind returned me to lay on the bed of blue melonia flowers, she approached me once more.

"Do you understand the vision?" asked she.

Unable to lie, I replied, "No, I do not."

"The vision is of things which have already come to pass. The vision may be unclear now, but with time, understanding shall come. You only need listen."

I listened, and as I lay among the blue melonia flowers, again I heard the faint whisper of a promise: *It is well. I am with you. I will always be with you.* And my heart was comforted by these words.

THE THIRD VISION

Again, I was swept up by a third great wind, and my soul was troubled, for I perceived another vision was to come, but still, I was yet to understand the first two which had been shown to me. Then cried I with my eyes closed, "Alas, it worries my soul to see these things; for, in my heart, I know they are significant, but in my mind, they are little more than fables."

My feet were placed on solid ground, and I opened my eyes to find that I had been returned to the top of the oak tree for a second time.

The man with sun-kissed skin and silver locks stared at me through piercing blue eyes, and I knew in my heart that it had now been two times and times and times again. And the man said, "Do not try to understand what your eyes perceive, for it is with the heart one truly sees. These visions may be unclear now, but understanding shall come. You only need listen. So listen with your ears and hear with your heart, and you shall perceive the true meaning of the things you see."

So I listened, and I watched, and I saw the entire land consumed by fire. And I perceived that the fire came up from the pit of the earth to consume it. And the fire was cruel and its flames were harsh, and it scorched the land and burned up the people, along with their possessions and their livestock. And all were burned up by this fire until only ash remained.

And I wept for the people and the land, for they had been consumed by a fire so cruel and a flame so harsh, and there was nothing left but ashes.

Overcome with despair, I rent my clothing and cried out to the sky and the sea and the land, and to the man upon the tree who was nameless and timeless and faceless; "O, but had we seen the flames rise up from the pit of the earth, then perhaps we could have saved those which are now lost."

Then spake the man with sun-kissed skin and greying locks and piercing blue eyes, "Flames to ashes, earth to dust[1]."

And I perceived not the meaning of his words, but hid them in my heart until such a time as understanding would come. And the man called the great flame *Sor-Azarael*, the meaning of which is *Destroyer of Many;* for it had risen from the pit of the earth and consumed the land and all that was upon it, save the great oak tree and the river which the girl with golden eyes gave her body to in order that it may flow.

The nameless and timeless and faceless man with sun-kissed skin and silver locks and piercing blue eyes blew upon the land, and a soft wind stirred the ashes of the fallen. The ashes rose and rose until they reached the stars and the people that dwelt among them.

Then the people taken up to the stars by the Great Wind, Oragon, cried out with a loud cry and descended to the land,

---

1. The phrase *Flames to ashes; Earth to dust,* was originally discovered in an ancient text found within Siriyghar, the ancient city of the gods, discovered by the rebels when fleeing the Rowanov Dragon Army during the Nissien Uprising.

but some remained among the stars. And those that remained wept for those who descended, for those who descended to the land did not know that once their feet touched the ground, they would ascend to the stars no more.

And on touching the land, those that descended realised what they had lost, and they were filled with sorrow and beat their chests and stomped their feet and wailed. And the stomping of their feet stirred up the ashes, and shook the ashes into the sea.

Then the people taken into the sea by the Great Wave, Honohley, cried out with a loud cry and ascended to the land, but some remained beneath the waves. And those that remained wept for those who ascended to the land, for those who ascended to the land did not know that once their feet touched the ground, they would descend beneath the waves no more. And on touching the land, those that ascended realised what they had lost, and they were filled with sorrow and beat their chests and stomped their feet and wailed.

Both those that had descended from the stars and those that had ascended from the waves were kind and would not that their brethren suffer their fate. So they came together as one, and bound the earth by their blood and by the ashes of the fallen, and they sealed the land forever in a pact to not take from anyone else what Oragon and Honohley had given.

Thus those that had descended from the stars and those that had ascended from the waves cultivated the land once more, starting from the river which the girl with golden eyes had granted her body in order that it may flow. And the soul of the girl with golden eyes restored the land and all that was upon it, for her soul healed the land through the waters of the river. And once the land was healed did the people begin their quest to return to the depths and ascend to the heavens.

But those that had remained in the stars and those that had remained in the sea were both cruel and harsh, and they came together, each in their own domain, and pledged never to let the people of the land return to the depths or ascend to the heavens. Thus, those beneath the waves would lie in wait to lure and drown the people of the land who travelled by sea. And these cruel people of the sea were called sirens. And the sirens drowned tens and thousands.

The Altars by the Sea

Those who had ascended from the depths came together as one and offered prayers and supplications to the guardians of the sea; for they quickly realised that the sirens would not that they return to Hinansho, that great city beneath the waves.

Therefore, they built altars upon the shore and sang praises to the elders who ruled over the Eastern Sea. And their names were Lola and Santiano. And the elder, Lola, led the armies of the Eastern Sea[2], while Santiano watched their borders, where the waters of the known world met the ocean. To these elders, the people of the land that had ascended from the depths gave offerings of first fruits and fine wine, and they appeased the sirens of the Eastern Sea.

Thus the people of the land who ascended from the depths said unto the elders who dwelt beneath the waves; "O, great

---

2. The Eastern Sea is now known as Aremamers.

elders who swim among the waves, hearken unto us and heed our cries; and let us return to our home, to our former dwelling, to Hinansho, the Great City beneath the waves."

To this, the elder, Lola, replied, "Brethren who now walk the land, I and my armies shall cease our drowning. But your request is one that even Santiano and I cannot fulfil. For such decisions lie outside of our power. Now, therefore, look elsewhere for aid. And if you or yours once again try to descend to the depths, my armies shall drown you without mercy."

Then, the people who had ascended to the land turned their faces to the North. Upon the coast, they built two altars: one to the elder, Sofina, and the other to the elder, Gadriel, who ruled over the Northern waters. The people of the land called these waters the Diamond Sea, for the blue-green of the waters resembled the Siren's eyes, and the waters oft sparkled like diamonds when the sun reached the horizon.

Unto the elders Gadriel and Sofina, the people offered songs of praise with the rising and setting sun. This, they did for three days and three nights, and the elders of the Northern Sea were appeased, and they ceased their drowning.

Thus the people of the land who ascended from the depths said unto the elders who dwelt beneath the waves; "O, great elders who walk within the deep, hearken unto us and heed our cries; and let us return to our home, to our former dwelling, to Hinansho, the Great City in the depths."

To this, the elder, Gadriel, said, "Brethren who have bonded with the soil, it is outside of our power to grant you this mercy. Now, set your faces south; to Moreto, Prince of the Sea and Ruler of Hinansho. Peradventure, he might look favourably on you and not smite you where you stand."

So the people who ascended to the land set their faces south, and upon the coast, they built a great altar to Moreto, Prince of the Sea, and to his siren bride. And for ten days, they offered prayers and supplications to the Siren Prince.

To him, they offered praise; and worship; and first fruits and good wine; and gold and silver and jewels of great price. For ten days and nights, they raised their voices and cried out to the sea, but the waters were silent.

The people who had ascended from the depths hungered and tired, and in the heat of the sun, grew frustrated and turned on one another. Thus, the people slew each other on the shore, until their blood ran into the sea.

Then rose Moreto, Prince of the Sea and Ruler of Hinansho, riding on a great wave. He wore shells in his hair and pearls around his neck, and bore a double-ended spear in his right hand and a huge shell horn in his left.

On seeing him, the people of the land ceased their warring. All bowed their faces to the earth in reverence towards him and his siren bride who rode beside him upon the wave.

The Siren Prince raised his voice and spake unto them, saying, "People of the land who walk upon the surface; who abandoned their charge within the sea and bonded themselves to the soil; I have heard your request, for the noise of your supplication is bothersome, and your offerings pollute the waters. Yet, your cries have touched the heart of my beloved bride and she has besought me to answer.

"Hear ye all this day, and hearken to my words: Though you are children of the sea, you forsook your calling and in turn lost the gifts given to you by the Great Wave, Honohley. Therefore, from henceforth, the soil shall be your heritage, the surface, your home. And should you try to return to the depths, my legion shall drown you with no mercy or remorse.

"But because you are children of the sea, and because my beloved bride wishes it, I shall grant you this favour: if ever you are struck down or in desperate need of aid, you shall send down an offering to Hinansho, and I shall hear and come to your aid."

"And what shall this offering be?" asked the people.

"Blood," said the Siren Prince. "As the moon draws the tide, so also shall the blood of a child of the sea draw me to the surface. And the blood which was spilled shall speak to me, and I shall hearken unto it. And I shall ascend from the depths to avenge it and slay all who played a part in spilling it."

Thus, the Siren Prince returned with his bride to the Great City beneath the waves, and all who gathered upon the shore dispersed, vowing to never call upon the Siren Prince, for the cost was too great, and they would be destroyed by his wrath.

The people of the land who had descended from the sky and wished to return to the stars grew trees of great heights, tall enough to rival small mountains. But they could not ascend by living in the treetops. So the people who had descended to the land cried out to those who had remained among the stars, but the stars were silent, for the people who had remained among the stars would not that those who had descended to the land should once more ascend to the heavens.

And the people who remained among the stars called those who had descended to the land by the name *Fallen*; for they had left their heavenly estate and abandoned their charge among the stars, and thus, had lost the gifts granted to them by the Great Wind, Oragon.

The First Tower

The Fallen, not perceiving that their pleas had been ignored, came together and said, "I perceive that our brethren among the stars do not hear our cries. Come, let us now build a tower to reach the heavens. And let us erect a tower that will cry out to the elders among the stars." For there were seven elders among those who remained among the stars.

So, the Fallen built a tower. This monolith was built in the south-eastern corner of the land, tall as the trees of the Fitonby Forest. And they built a tower with its point to the sky beneath the star of the elder, Uulshaa, and cried out day and night for seven suns. But Uulshaa did not heed their cries for help. For, unbeknownst to the Fallen, the elder, Uulshaa, and the other six elders who remained among the stars did not want their fallen brethren to once again ascend to the sky.

And after the sun had risen seven times, the Fallen said, "We perceive that Uulshaa, that great and mighty elder of the South-East, does not hear our cries. Come, let us now build a second tower to reach the heavens. And let us erect a tower that will cry out to the elder, Suri Onash."

So many of the Fallen went north, towards Bleclif. But some remained steadfast beneath the star of the elder, Uulshaa; and they that remained built themselves homes among the trees of the Fitonby Forest and cried unto the elder, Uulshaa, day and night.

They which remained numbered one thousand, seven hundred and fifty.

The Second Tower

The rest of the Fallen went unto Bleclif, and there they built a second tower. This monolith was built in the north-eastern corner of the land, high as the Bleclif mountains. And they built a tower with its point to the sky beneath the star of the elder, Suri Onash, and cried out day and night for seven suns.

But Suri Onash did not heed their cries for help. For, unbeknownst to the Fallen, the elder, Suri Onash, and the other six elders who remained among the stars did not want the Fallen to once again ascend to the sky.

And after the sun had risen seven times, the Fallen that were in Bleclif said, "We perceive that Suri Onash, that wise and just elder of the North-East, does not hear our cries. Come, let us now build a third tower to reach the heavens. And let us erect a tower that will cry out to the elder, Mi-Kalia."

So the Fallen travelled west towards the place now called Retnesto. But some remained within the Bleclif Mountains and cried out to Suri Onash fortnightly. And among them which remained was the one called Ahazret; a mighty man of valour who was giant in stature. And those that remained in the Bleclif Mountains numbered themselves, and they were three thousand and twenty-four.

The Third Tower

And those who went west towards Retnesto built a third tower. This monolith was built in the north of the land, rising and rising and rising. And they built a tower with its point to the sky beneath the star of the elder, Mi-Kalia, and cried out day and night for seven suns.

And the elder, Mi-Kalia, looked down upon her brethren and had compassion for them. But because of the agreement between Mi-Kalia and the six other elders who dwelt among the stars and did not want their fallen brethren to once again ascend to the skies, Mi-Kalia did not heed their cries for help. Instead, she let her star shine bright and blue, that the Fallen might know that their cries had been heard.

Seeing this, the Fallen said, "We perceive that our cries have reached the heavens, for Mi-Kalia, the kind and compassionate elder of the North, has given us a sign. Behold, her star shines blue and bright; brighter than any star in the heavens." And the Fallen were encouraged by the sign, and they called this star *Crown of the North*; for the star of Mi-Kalia shone bright and blue, that the Fallen might know that their cries had been heard.

But the elders who dwelt among the stars and did not want their fallen brethren to return to the skies were greatly troubled by this, and they came together and vowed a vow, and strengthened the vow they had previously vowed not to let the Fallen once again ascend to the stars.

After the sun had risen seven times, the Fallen said once more, "Come, let us now build a fourth tower to reach the heavens.

And let us erect a tower that will cry out to the elder, Yameer. Peradventure, he may look pitiably on us and help us ascend once more."

But many among the Fallen said, "Nay, let us remain beneath the Crown of the North; for the elder, Mi-Kalia has heard us once, and in time, she will answer and restore us to our heavenly estate."

Thus, there was a divide among the people, and some went west, towards the place called Pavos, but many remained in Retnesto, beneath the Crown of the North. And they that remained were numbered at seven thousand, seven hundred and fifty-four.

One among those that remained bore a son in the night. Then the mother went to sleep, and when she awoke, the child was gone from his cot. Many of the Fallen wept, for the child was the first to be born among them since they had descended to the land. But some said, "It is well. The child has been taken up by the elders who dwell among the stars; for he is innocent of our transgression and should not share in our suffering."

Thus, the mother named her missing child *Duriel*, meaning *the one who ascends*; and she mourned him for a fortnight.

The Fourth Tower

The Fallen that went west towards Pavos built a fourth tower. This monolith was built in the north-western corner of the land, high as the hills of Pavos. And they built a tower with its point to the sky beneath the star of the elder, Yameer, and cried out day and night for seven suns.

But Yameer did not heed their cries for help. For, unbeknownst to the Fallen, the elder, Yameer, and the other elders who remained among the stars did not want their fallen brethren to return to the stars; and because of the sign Mi-Kalia had given, they had vowed a vow, and strengthened the vow they had previously vowed to not let the Fallen once again ascend to the sky.

And after the sun had risen seven times, the Fallen that were gathered in Pavos said, "We perceive that Yameer, that fierce and noble elder of the West, does not heed our cries. Come, let us now build a fifth tower to reach the heavens. And let us erect a tower that will cry out to the elder, Josadom."

Again, some refused, wishing to make their home in the north-western corner of the land. And they that remained beneath the star of the elder, Yameer, numbered three thousand and seventy.

The Fifth Tower

The rest of the Fallen travelled south, towards the place now called Wodbuton, and there they built a fifth tower. This monolith was built in the south-western corner of the land, as wide as the shores of Wodbuton. And they built a tower with its point to the sky beneath the star of the elder, Josadom, and cried out day and night for seven suns.

But Josadom also did not heed their cries for help. And the Fallen began to perceive that the elder, Josadom, and the other six elders who remained among the stars did not want those who had descended to the land to once again ascend to the sky.

After the sun had risen seven times, the Fallen said, "We perceive that Josadom, that keen and clever elder of the South, does not heed our cries. For we have wept for seven suns upon seven suns and the elders who dwell among the stars do not come to our aid. We know they hear us, as was confirmed by the sign from Mi-Kalia, so why do they turn away when we call?"

The people that dwelt among the stars were vexed by the sayings of those of the land, and were doubly vexed by the sign Mi-Kalia had given them. And the people that dwelt among the stars said, "Let us slay this traitor in our midst, for it is not above her to send aid to the people of the land when no one watches."

When the elders that dwelt among the stars heard the proclamation of the people of the sky, they agreed that Mi-Kalia was too kind and would someday betray the vow which they vowed; but they would not slay her, for she was numbered as one of them. Instead, the elders that dwelt among the stars took Mi-Kalia and bound her hands and feet with fetters of steel and pewter and stone.

Thus, she was bound by fetters that could not be broken and could never betray the vow which they vowed to not let their fallen brethren return to the sky.

When the Fallen that were gathered in Wodbuton perceived that the elders heard their cries, they said unto one another, "Come, let us now build a sixth tower to reach the heavens. And let us erect a tower that will cry out to the elder, Tai. For if the other elders refuse to heed us, then Tai shall go against their agreement and we are sure to be saved."

They said this because Tai, that quick and cunning elder, would surely find a way to outwit the other elders who dwelt among the stars.

And the elders who dwelt among the stars heard this and were filled with fear, and grumbled among themselves, saying; "It is true that Tai is quick and cunning, and would surely find a way to outwit us all without betraying the vow which we vowed to not let the people who had descended to the land return to the sky."

And Tai smiled a smile that meant their words were true.

The Sixth Tower

The Fallen sent word to their brethren across the land saying, "Lo, we shall now travel to the Peaks of Penzan, and there we shall build a tower beneath the star of the elder, Tai, and we shall beseech him for seven suns. And if he does answer us with signs in the heavens, then we shall conclude that the elders who dwell among the stars do hear us, but choose to turn deaf ears to our pleas."

So they besought a thousand and thirty of their number to remain beneath the star of the elder, Josadom, and they of the Fallen which travelled east towards the place called Penzan numbered five thousand strong; and there they built a sixth and final tower. This monolith was built in the south of the land, on top of the Penzan Peaks. And they built a tower with its point to the sky beneath the star of the elder, Tai. And there, five thousand voices rose as one, crying out day and night for seven suns.

And the people which dwelt among the stars trembled, for they feared the elder, Tai, and what he might do. And they said, "Let us take Tai and slay him, for he will surely undo all we have done to keep the Fallen from returning to the sky. And let us keep our plans secret from the elders, for they will surely try to stop us as they stopped us from slaying the traitor, Mi-Kalia."

So the people which dwelt among the stars assembled in secret and sought to slay Tai.

A New Vow

Alone in his palace upon his star in the south, the elder, Tai, watched the land from the heavens and smiled; for he knew that the people which dwelt among the stars sought to slay him in secret.

For three days and nights, Tai feigned ignorance. And when the people who dwelt among the stars approached, Tai turned around and slew them.

In one night, he slew tens and thousands, until the star upon which he dwelt was steeped in red. Then said he, "On this day, I have slain they that wished to slay me, and by their blood, I vow a new vow: each day that the cries of the people on the land reach my ears, I shall slay tens and thousands of the people who dwell among the stars, for they have betrayed me."

The elders who dwelt among the stars said, "Have your way," for they believed that the Fallen would cry out for seven suns, just as they had done before, and then Tai would no longer slay those who dwelt among the stars and his retribution would be complete.

And so, for seven suns, Tai slew tens and thousands with his great sword, and the people who dwelt among the stars fell as blazing balls of light which shot across the night sky.

All the people of the land saw this wonder and perceived it as a sign. And the Fallen cried out for seven suns, and seven more suns, and then seven suns more.

And the elders who dwelt among the stars fell to their knees and besought Tai to repent of his vow; but he would not, for it was true that the people who dwelt among the stars had betrayed him, and his retribution was just, though grave. So Tai slew tens and thousands for each day that the cries of his fallen brethren reached his ears.

With fear and trembling, the elders who dwelt among the stars besought Tai once more, saying, "What will make you repent of your vow and have mercy on the people who dwell among the stars?"

To this, Tai replied, "O elders and people who dwell among the stars, three requests have I. These three are the only conditions upon which I will stay my retribution, once fulfilled."

And the people said, "We are listening."

The Curse of the Elders

Then spake Tai unto the people and the elders that dwelt among the stars; "For my first request: unbind Mi-Kalia, and let no harm come to her."

And the people and the elders that dwelt among the stars said, "That, we shall do."

So the elders took Mi-Kalia and freed her hands and feet from their fetters of steel and pewter and stone, thus Mi-Kalia was free once more. And Mi-Kalia returned to Tai's side, for she loved him greatly and was freed from her shackles because of him.

Then spake Tai again, saying, "For my second request: grant to the Fallen that they may sprout wings and soar among the clouds, for they shall thus believe that we who dwell among the stars have heard and answered their cries and they shall beseech me no more."

And the people and the elders that dwelt among the stars said, "That, we shall do." But they perceived not that Tai, that quick and cunning elder, trusted them not and requested this of them to test what was in their hearts.

Because the people which dwelt amongst the stars were cruel, they spoke harshly towards their fallen brethren, and cursed them, that they may become beasts with wings that would carry them to soar amongst the clouds. And the people which dwelt amongst the stars cursed the Fallen with a curse, saying, "Now shall you become beasts and sprout wings from your backs, that you may ascend to the clouds. But let these wings have no covering, that they may be scorched by the heat of the sun."

Thus, the Fallen who at that time besought the elders that dwelt among the stars were cursed with a curse. And they became great hideous beasts, and sprouted wings of flesh and bone, but no feathers covered them. And they were scorched by the sun as they ascended to the clouds. And their skin grew hard and leathery, and cracked under the strain of use, and they fell from the clouds and would have died.

But Mi-Kalia, that kind and compassionate elder, took pity on them, and she granted them scales like bone and steel and stone that they may withstand the heat of the sun.

So the cursed among the Fallen were covered in scales: some white like bone, some grey like steel, and some red like clay. And they withstood the heat and did not fall to their deaths.

Once again, the Fallen perceived this as another sign from the elder, Tai, and they cried out once more unto him. And for each day the Fallen cried out, Tai, that quick and cunning elder, slew tens and thousands of the people that dwelt among the stars; for Tai knew and perceived that the people that dwelt among the stars were cruel and harsh and had meant evil upon their fallen brethren, though the Fallen perceived it not.

And the people and the elders that dwelt among the stars besought Tai once more to cease his slaughter, for Tai slaughtered many with his great sword. And the great sword was named Azarael, after the Great Flame that had burned the land to ash.

Then spake Tai to the elders and people who dwelt among the stars, "Did you think it wise to curse the people of the land so? For I am a quick and cunning elder, and I perceive that treachery lies deep in your hearts. So, for this reason, I shall stay my third and final request, and my retribution shall continue. For had it not been for the kindness of Mi-Kalia, you would have slain our fallen brethren. As it stands, they have become like beasts upon the land."

So, Tai stayed his third and final request; and as the Fallen cried out to him, he slew the people that dwelt among the stars with his great sword, Azarael, for Tai's wrath was great. And he slew tens and thousands and tens of thousands, and the heavens rained lights, so the people of the land cried out some more.

Then the people and elders that dwelt among the stars came together and said, "Let us beseech the elder, Mi-Kalia, that she might intercede on our behalf; for she is a kind and compassionate elder, and the elder, Tai, loves her greatly."

So the people and elders that dwelt among the stars besought Mi-Kalia, that she might have mercy and intercede on their behalf.

Mi-Kalia was moved with compassion for the people and elders that dwelt among the stars, and she besought Tai on their behalf, saying; "O Tai, you quick and cunning elder, heed my plea and look upon my face. For I know that the transgression of the people is great and your wrath burns hotter than the flames of Sor-Azarael, but I know that there is kindness in your heart, as in times past, you have looked upon me with great kindness. I beseech you, O elder, that you look upon me once more and stay your wrath."

Thus, Tai, that quick and cunning elder, looked upon Mi-Kalia, and his wrath was stayed when he beheld her, for he loved Mi-Kalia greatly.

But the Fallen raised their voices louder and cried out to the elder, Tai, and his eyes were turned from Mi-Kalia and his wrath renewed once more. And for each day the people of the land cried out, Tai slew tens and thousands of the people that dwelt among the stars.

Then the people and elders that dwelt among the stars came together and said, "We perceive that Tai, that quick and cunning elder, loves Mi-Kalia greatly, for when he beheld her, his wrath was stayed. Now let us turn the heart of Mi-Kalia away from the elder, Tai, that his heart be destroyed, and his will, broken."

This did the people and elders both agree to do. So they approached Mi-Kalia once more, and when Mi-Kalia turned to listen, they said, "We come with a grave matter, O kind and compassionate elder of the South. We perceive that the elder, Tai, loves you not. For you required a thing of him and gave he not that which you requested."

Then said Mi-Kalia unto them, "Do you take my kindness for weakness and my compassion for foolishness? Do you think I have forgotten who it was that bound my hands and feet in fetters of stone and pewter and iron, and who it was that set me free? And though many among you wish to slay me, for whose sake is it that your hand has been stayed against me? I know in my heart that Tai loves me with a great love, but he gave me not that which I requested, for it was not mine to request. It was not my transgression which needed forgiveness, nor my punishment which needed mercy. Yet, Tai stayed his hand when he beheld me."

On hearing Mi-Kalia's words, the people and elders that dwelt among the stars fell to their knees and bowed their faces before her and wept; for their plan had failed and Mi-Kalia had not been deceived. But Mi-Kalia, that kind and compassionate elder, was moved by their mourning, and she raised a hand and silenced them all saying, "I shall return to the elder, Tai; I shall beseech him once more on your behalf. And I shall request what he requires of you in order that his second condition be fulfilled."

Thus, the people and elders were grateful and thanked Mi-Kalia. And the hearts of some were moved and a deep love for her was stirred up in them and they repented that they had sought to harm her. But some repented not, for they hated Mi-Kalia with a deep hatred because she was beautiful and kind, and because Tai loved her greatly.

Then Mi-Kalia returned to Tai and said, "Pray tell, my love; what will you have the other elders do to fulfil your second condition?"

Tai smiled a smile, for he perceived that the elder he loved, in her kindness, was truly moved with compassion for the people who dwelt among the stars, despite their plot against her. So he said, "Come, my love. Lie with me tonight, and I shall consider your request."

So Mi-Kalia lay with him, for she loved him with a deep love. And when morning came, Tai said unto her, "I have considered your request, my love, and have chosen to ignore it. For our brethren are of a wicked sort, and evil dwells in their hearts."

"But surely, not all are evil," said Mi-Kalia. "Surely, some can be saved."

"Nay," said Tai. "All are evil; both they and we. For we abandoned our brethren and vowed a vow to not let them ascend. It is because of us that our fallen brethren now suffer and die; because we do nothing while they cry unto us day and night."

Moved by his words, Mi-Kalia laid her head on his chest and wept, for it was a true thing he had spoken. And she decided in her heart to help the people of the land without breaking the vow she had vowed and strengthened.

And when the day was far spent, she rose and dressed and went out to meet the other elders and the people who dwelt among the stars.

The people who dwelt among the stars rejoiced greatly at the sight of her, for none of their brethren had been slain that night while Tai lay with her, and they believed him convinced to stay his wrath. But Mi-Kalia said, "It is not so. The elder, Tai, has denied my request."

Thus, the remaining elders who dwelt among the stars perceived that Tai had ceased his slaughter while he lay with Mi-Kalia, for her cries stopped his ears to the pleas of the people on the land, and her body blinded his eyes to their supplication. Then said they unto her, "Mi-Kalia, O kind and compassionate elder; enter once again into his chamber and beseech him, and lie with him for another night."

Seeing the hope and fear in the eyes of the people who dwelt among the stars, Mi-Kalia said, "This I shall do, that none of you may be slain."

And even more of the people who dwelt among the stars came to love her, for they knew not that she loved Tai greatly and believed that she offered herself up to him, in order to save them.

So Mi-Kalia went in unto Tai and laid with him once, and twice, and thrice more. And when seven nights had passed and none of the people who dwelt among the stars had been slain, the Fallen ceased their cries unto the elder, Tai, for they had seen no sign in the heavens for seven days.

Thus, the Fallen said, "Come, let us now build a seventh tower to reach the heavens. And let us erect a tower that will cry out to the elder, Carmen."

So some of the people of the land that had descended from the stars went north towards Catbury. But many would not leave, for they perceived that the elder, Tai, had heard their call and they believed he would surely deliver them. So some went and some stayed. And they which believed on the elder, Tai, numbered five thousand, but they which travelled towards Catbury were few as three hundred and twenty-six; thus they had not the strength to erect a tower.

So the people of the land that ventured towards Catbury built a tall bridge and cried out to the elder Carmen. And they called the bridge *Garua*. To this day, the stones of the Garua remain, holding the land together as one even after the land was split by the Great Fall when the elder, Tai, fell from the stars.

The great wind returned me to lay on the bed of blue melonia flowers.

"Do you understand the vision?" asked she, appearing before me.

"Once again, I do not," answered I. "And my heart is sorely grieved by this; for I see things which I cannot fathom, and my body is left weary, yet my mind remains unfruitful."

She sat beside me, and cupped my face in her hands, and said, "The vision is of things which have already come to pass. The vision may be unclear now, but with time, understanding shall come. You only need listen."

So, once more, I listened, and as I lay among the blue melonia flowers, I heard the familiar words of a promise: *It is well. I am with you. I will always be with you.* And my heart was comforted by these words, though my mind remained restless.

THE FOURTH VISION

I was swept up by a fourth great wind, and I perceived another vision was to come. And though my soul was troubled, I determined in my heart not to seek understanding with my mind, but to listen with my heart.

So, as the great wind returned me to the top of the oak tree for a third time, I said to the man with sun-kissed skin and silver hair and piercing blue eyes, "What shall be this great vision? For I perceive it has been but a time since I last stood atop this great oak tree."

"Alas, my friend," said he; "only through your eyes can I see the visions which you see, for it is from your mind and not with my eyes that I perceive them. Now, listen, and watch, and we shall perceive the last vision of the past which cannot be unwritten."

So I listened, and I watched, and I saw signs painted in the night skies: a bear; a fox; a dragon; an archer; a wolf; an owl; a phoenix. And these signs were used by the people of the land for signs and for times and for seasons. And these signs were called the *zodiakh* signs.

Thus, the people of the land mapped out the heavens using the signs in the stars, and they called this map the *zodiakh*. And those born under each sign were given names befitting their sign, that they may embody the attributes thereof.

For many days, the elder, Tai, lay with his love; and he taught her many things about the stars and the people that dwelt among them. But the elder, Mi-Kalia, remained troubled by his previous words, for she saw the truth: that she and all those who dwelt among the stars had done a great evil against their fallen brethren. And she knew not how to rectify it, for she had sworn an oath and strengthened the oath which she had sworn never to help the Fallen return to the stars.

Seeing that her countenance had fallen, Tai spake unto her saying, "What troubles you, my love?"

And to this, Mi-Kalia said, "I would that we right the wrong we have done to our fallen brethren, but I know not how."

"Then come," said Tai, "and I shall teach you what you must do."

So Mi-Kalia followed Tai out into the night. There, Tai drew a symbol in the sky. And it was that of a fox. Then spake he unto Mi-Kalia, "Come now, I have taught you a great many things these past few days; one of which being how to speak to the people of the land. Now send a vision down, that they may see it and perceive what the sign in the sky means."

This Mi-Kalia did. And she sent a vision down to the people of the land, and spake to them of harvest; of fruitful grain and bounteous crop, and baskets overflowing. And the people of the land, seeing the sign in the sky, and perceiving the vision, conferred among themselves, saying, "What is this sign in the heavens? And what is this vision we see? Is this from the elders who dwell among the stars?"

Then Tai said unto Mi-Kalia, "Make your star shine bright and blue, that they may know this sign is from you."

So Mi-Kalia made her star shine bright and blue, and the people of the land perceived that the sign was from her. And they of the Fallen which remained in the tower at Retnesto built altars beneath her star; and they worshipped her and offered up burnt offerings unto her. And Mi-Kalia was pleased by this, and she remained upon her star, painting signs in the heavens and sending visions to the land. And the people of the land loved her and hailed her, and worshipped her as a god, for she taught them and helped them greatly.

And Tai returned unto his own star. And when the Fallen that remained beneath his star cried out, he turned and took his great sword, Azarael, and slew tens and thousands of the people who dwelt among the stars. Each night he slew them without pity or remorse, for he knew they had sent Mi-Kalia unto him to stay his hand.

Seeing that the stars once again fell from the sky, the people of the land praised and worshipped him, and besought him for a sign. So he painted the heavens with falling stars and sent a vision to the land that they may know that he hears and he answers, and he avenges those who call upon him.

Thus, the elder, Tai, came to be known as the Avenger; the Warrior God who fights the battles of all who call upon him. And the elder, Mi-Kalia, came to be known as the kind and compassionate god; the one who provides for and protects all who call upon her.

And when the other elders learned that Mi-Kalia was called the Great Mother, and Tai, the Father of the Night, their wicked hearts were filled with jealousy. And they came together and said, "How shall we put a stop to this?"

Then the elder, Carmen, stepped forward and said, "It is not good that a god be so separate from her people. Now, therefore, let us send Mi-Kalia down to the land, that she may walk among those who worship her." This Carmen spake, for she was the most jealous of them all; for where the other elders had received towers in their names, she had received only a bridge, and those that called out to her numbered few.

But the other elders said, "Nay. We have done a wicked thing once and twice; we will not do it a third time, for the wrath of Tai is great. Therefore, we shall not provoke him again."

"Then let us send Tai down to the land," said Carmen. "With him on the land, the bloodshed in the heavens shall cease. Furthermore, Mi-Kalia shall be powerless without his covering, and we can do with her as we please."

While the other elders considered her words, the elder, Josadom, said, "Let us make no hasty decisions, for Tai is a quick and cunning elder and he will surely outwit us if we act rashly. Let us each consider the matter and reconvene at a later date to decide."

The other elders nodded their agreement, and when they had all departed, Josadom went unto Tai and said, "I am wary of Carmen. I perceive she is bitter and bears a grudge against the one you love. For, as the elders gathered today to grumble against you and your love, she spoke of a plot to send Mi-Kalia down to the land to walk among the people. I perceive it is her hope that

Mi-Kalia will be stuck down below and lose her divine gifts from Oragon like our brethren who descended to the land."

Tai smiled, for he knew that the land had drunk its fill and been bound by the people of the land so it would not take from anyone else the gifts bestowed upon them by the Great Wind, Oragon, or the Great Wave, Honohley. Furthermore, he knew it was Carmen's hope that, with Mi-Kalia gone, she would reign on the Crown of the North in Mi-Kalia's stead.

Then he spake unto Josadom saying, "Why tell me this? Why betray the trust of the other elders who conspire against us?"

"Alas, my friend, I am a grumbler and a coward. I do not seek to raise my hand against you, for your wrath burns like the flames of Sor-Azarael, and your vengeance knows no bounds. I know that if Mi-Kalia is harmed in any way, you will have retribution—be it in one year or one thousand. I do not wish to meet my end at your blade. Thus, I propose this; that we be friends. True friends."

"Is there anything true about you?" asked Tai.

"You wound me, friend," said Josadom. "Were it not for our friendship, then I would not tell you that Carmen still bears a grudge against you for rejecting her. And she bears a deeper hatred for Mi-Kalia because she is your love. Furthermore, it was because of your sign in the sky that only few of the people on the land went on to build a monolith in her name. So few they were that they could only manage a bridge, and not a great tower like the ones erected in our names. To add to it, that you parade Mi-Kalia across the heavens and make her name great upon the earth is vexing, even to me. Are we not all elders? Are we not all great?"

Then Tai said, "Even in the heavens, some stars burn brighter. Mi-Kalia's star burns the brightest, for she is kind and compassionate, and has the purest heart. Even I do not seek to outshine her, for I know I cannot. I know you are a keen and clever elder, Josadom. Let us each now give heed to the duties which we alone can perform."

"And what might my duty be?" asked Josadom.

"You are clever," said Tai, "You shall perceive it soon."

So Josadom departed from Tai's presence, and considered Tai's words, and gave his mind and heart to figuring out what duty it was that only he could fulfil.

Then Tai went unto Mi-Kalia and spake unto her saying, "Come now, my love. I perceive that our fellow elders grow jealous of your greatness and now plot among themselves to see your destruction. For your star shines bright in the heavens, and your name is greatly praised upon the land. Now, therefore, tarry with me a while, that they might remember whose heart you hold and whom it is that shall smite them if they raise a hand against you."

So Mi-Kalia went with him, and the two returned to his star in the south. And while Mi-Kalia remained upon his star, Tai's hand was stayed against his brethren, and none of those who dwelt among the stars was slain. Thus, many of the people who dwelt among the stars grew to love Mi-Kalia, and they too hailed her and worshipped her as a god; for only a true god could stay Tai's hand.

Seeing this, the other elders' hearts were filled with wrath, for their jealousy was great; yet they could not hurt Mi-Kalia for fear of Tai's retribution.

And when many days had passed, that keen and clever elder, Josadom, returned unto Tai in secret and said, "Many days have passed, dear friend, and still I fail to perceive what task it is that only I can perform." On seeing Mi-Kalia, the elder, Josadom, turned to her with a bow and greeted her as the people of the land did. (Some of the people who dwelt among the stars and hailed Mi-Kalia as a god had adopted that greeting.)

This pleased Tai greatly, and he spake unto Josadom, saying, "Come, friend. Tarry with us a while, and perhaps wisdom might look favourably upon thee."

So Josadom remained on the star to the south and enquired many things of the Great Mother. This, the elder, Tai, had done to occupy Mi-Kalia. And when the Fallen which remained beneath his star cried unto him, he turned and slew tens and thousands of the people who dwelt among the stars. But all those that dwelt among the stars who revered and honoured the elder, Mi-Kalia, Tai did not slay.

For many days, Josadom remained, and for many days, Tai slew the people who dwelt among the stars until those who opposed the elder, Mi-Kalia, numbered few. And they that dwelt among the stars grew fearful, for the other elders had not fulfilled Tai's condition to stay his hand, and they feared that once those opposed to the elder, Mi-Kalia, were slain, the elder, Tai, would turn his wrath upon them.

So they went to the other elders in secret and pleaded with them to go unto Tai and intercede on their behalf. But the other elders would not, for fear; for they were numbered among those who did not revere Mi-Kalia.

Then Tai turned unto Josadom and said, "Depart from my star, that I might be with my love."

"Nay," said Josadom. "What great need do you have with Mi-Kalia that you must sequester her?"

"It is a private matter," said Tai. "One that pertains to my manly desires."

"Then we shall split her time in half, for there is still much I might learn from her. She shall teach me during the day, and you may be with her at night."

Tai shook his head and said, "Not so. I require her day as well as her night, for I must teach her to master the bow. Furthermore, I perceive the other elders conspire once more; go now, therefore, unto them and discover what wiles they weave. If your presence is missed, they will perceive you have tarried with Mi-Kalia, and they shall surely turn against you."

And when Mi-Kalia heard that there was contention between them for her sake, she said unto Josadom, "Do as the elder, Tai, has commanded. For, if your presence is indeed missed, the other elders will perceive that you have tarried with me a while, and they will surely turn against you. Furthermore, if this comes to pass, Tai shall not raise his hand to protect you; for he sent you away and you heeded him not."

So Josadom, bowing low, departed and went unto the other elders. And behold, they schemed a scheme to cast Mi-Kalia down to the land, that they might be rid of her. On learning this, Josadom's heart grew troubled, and he spake unto the other elders saying, "I fear such a twisted scheme is inspired by a darkness that does not belong among the stars. For this scheme which you scheme has its roots in hell, and shall surely be the destruction of all."

But the elder, Carmen, raised her voice and said, "Lo, you return to us from Mi-Kalia's bosom; and with your treacherous tongue, you spout lies in a bid to save her."

"Enough with your foolishness, Carmen," said Josadom. "Do you so desperately seek to possess Tai's heart that you would rip it out of his chest?"

"It is not his heart I seek; but his head," said Carmen.

"Then go to him and take it! Spare us all the trouble of endangering our world. Take up your axe, and let it strike true. And when you fail, we shall appoint another in your stead. For in your jealousy, you have grown foolish; and love has driven you mad."

Enraged, Carmen raised her axe to strike Josadom in the chest. But an arrow pierced her shoulder, and she cried out as she stumbled back and dropped her axe.

Josadom, perceiving that the arrow which had saved him was from the south, rose to his feet and said, "Behold, the elder, Tai, watches over the heavens, and the elder, Mi-Kalia, the land. And under their hand, all have prospered. Yet, we sit here and conspire against them."

Then said the great and mighty elder, Uulshaa, "Prospered, you say? The heavens have bled by Tai's blade. Once we outnumbered the sands of the southern beaches. Yet, Tai alone has dwindled us down to mere tens of thousands. Shall we then stay our hand until he drives us to the brink of extinction?"

"Nay, Uulshaa," said Josadom. "It was we who betrayed Tai's trust and set him on this path: first, by seeking to hurt Mi-Kalia; then by seeking to hurt our brethren who descended to the land—for his second request was that we grant a gift to the Fallen that they may know we hear and answer them. For is that not what it is to be a god? Yet, we harbour jealousy in our hearts towards Mi-Kalia because she has done what we would not. Except for Carmen, whose jealousy stems from Mi-Kalia being exalted by Tai."

Then Suri Onash, the wise and just elder, said, "What Josadom says is right. If we indeed were noble in our deeds, the people of the land would sing our praises. Now, we have vowed a vow and strengthened the vow which we have vowed never to let the people who descended to the land return to the sky. Therefore, let us send them signs, and give them visions of a future that is not yet written. And let us teach them to conduct themselves in a manner that benefits us. Let us teach some the secrets of the stars which they have forgotten, and grant others power from the heavens, just enough for signs and wonders, that they may perceive these and worship us.

"And each shall send down a vision, that all may believe. And the vision shall be one of a glorious end, a triumphal return to the stars; and this return shall be contingent on their obedience to the tenets each shall prescribe. Thus, we too shall each be gods over our own people, and we shall hold their salvation in our hands. And they shall hearken unto us and cease their crying unto the elder, Tai, and his second requirement may be fulfilled."

Hearing this, the other elders agreed to do as Suri Onash had instructed. But Carmen was wrought, for she perceived that the arrow that had pierced her shoulder had not come from Tai, but from Mi-Kalia. For when Tai fired an arrow, it was to slay.

The elders who dwelt among the stars did as they had purposed in their hearts to do. And each painted a sign in the heavens and sent down a vision to the people of the land and taught them many things.

In time, the people of the land who dwelt in the South-East, beneath the star of the elder, Uulshaa, saw the image of the bear in the stars above them. And for each night it shone in the sky, they that dwelt in the monolith within the Fitonby Forest dreamed dreams and saw visions of returning to their home in the sky.

And they were given five tenets[1] by the elder, Uulshaa, that they may obey these and, in time, see the vision come to fruition. And these tenets were, first: on honour and power. To wield power without honour is a fallacy, and gain ill-acquired is malfeasance.

Second: on keeping a home. First, there is family. It shall always be so. Each shall protect the other, and neither is greater than the other and no task is more highly esteemed for it is in working together that the family is kept whole.

Third: to settle disputes within three suns, lest the feuding parties incur his wrath and be sacrificed upon his altar.

---

1. A summary of the five tenets has been listed in this translation. Perhaps the Late Mother Yrnanon, in such dire a circumstance she found herself and Enacia in, decided it best to abbreviate in order to cover more pressing content before her passing. A complete translation of these tenets can be found at the end of this manuscript.

Fourth: on worship by offering a tenth portion of all increase, that the bastard and the orphan might find food, lodging, and work within his temple.

Fifth: that none enter into a marital union for financial gain. It is a vile thing to covet earthly treasures, and the fruit of such union is segregation and a breakdown of the community. Instead, let a man and woman be united in love. Thus, they shall become a family and lay with no other. And let each family be mindful of their sustenance; for children are a blessing, and must be treated as such.

Thus, the sign of the elder, Uulshaa, came to be known as Tradjehn, and Uulshaa, the Bear; for he was a great and mighty elder. And he taught his people to master crafts of wood and stone. And from him, they learned to build houses and cities and erect towers that reached up to the skies. And they learned to rule and to govern. And his people became the first advanced society.

And Tradjehn became the sign of the first planting season, for it shone in the South-East during the time of planting.

Then the people of the land who dwelt in the South-West, beneath the star of the elder, Josadom, saw the image of the fox in the stars above them. And for each night it shone in the sky, they that dwelt in the monolith on the shores of Wodbuton dreamed dreams and saw visions of a triumphal return to the stars, and of a glorious banquet prepared in their honour.

And they were given three tenets by the elder, Josadom, that they may obey these and in time, see the vision come to pass. First: to keep the balance, for there is a balance and the balance must be kept.

Second: to strike a bargain. Knowledge is precious, and the price thereof would be. To take, one must give in equal measure.

And third: to interpret the signs. For there are signs in the heavens of the things which shall be on the earth, and testimonies on dried bones of the things which have been.

Thus, the sign of the elder, Josadom, came to be known as Fusha, the Fox; and the elder, Josadom, was called the Fox God, for he was a keen and clever elder. He it was who taught his people to understand the past and to seek knowledge of the future. And from him they learned the signs of the stars and the earth and oracling and divination. And they were them that knew the stars and divined things through nature and bones.

And Fusha became the sign of the first harvest season, for it shone in the south-western sky during the time of the first harvest.

Then the people of the land who dwelt in the North-West, beneath the star of the elder, Yameer, saw the image of the dragon in the stars above them. And for each night it shone in the sky, they that dwelt in the monolith built high as the hills of Pavos[2] dreamed dreams and saw visions of being raptured into the stars and returning to their heavenly estate. And they were given four tenets by the elder, Yameer, that they may obey these and, in time, see the vision come to pass.

And these tenets were first; be mindful of all things, for an account will be required of you for all things under your charge.

Second: *Ki* is the soul, and the soul is in everything, and it is everything that is and everything that it is not. *Qudra* is the soul manifest beyond the flesh.

---

2. This tower is believed to have been located in what is now the Forest of Murah, as that entire region was considered to be part of Pavos before the Cursed Ones called the forest home.

Third: the control of *qudra* is conceived by desire and is birthed within the will.

Fourth: the use of *qudra* comes at a price.

Thus, the elder, Yameer, came to be known as the Great Wyrm or the Great Serpent; for he was a fierce and noble elder; and his sign in the sky was called Draken Meien. And this became the sign in the sky to mark the second planting season.

Yameer taught his people indulgence and ways of adorning themselves and embellishing their skin with colours to enhance their beauty. From him they learned the art of beautifying themselves and many ways by which to find pleasure, until they learned to master it, that it not rule over them. And when they had mastered restraint, he taught them to master the elements; and they were them that wielded the magic of the earth and the sky and the seas and flame.

Then the people of the land who dwelt on the Garua, beneath the star of the elder, Carmen, saw the image of an archer in the stars above them. And the Archer[3] was drawn with six different constellations, just as Mi-Kalia had painted six images in the skies.

For each night it shone in the sky, all the people of the land who cried out to her dreamed a dream and saw a vision. And the vision was of a glorious ascension to the heavens to reign far above all the people of the land and those that dwelt among the stars. And she gave them two tenets: the first, to open the Arkon

---

3. The Archer is made up of six asterisms which individually start to appear in the sky every 111 moons (years), until the sign of the Archer is complete.

Gates and free the Ancient[4] who slumbered beneath the earth, no matter the cost or consequence. And the second: to slay all who opposed this vision.

And she taught them to war and to slay, and to draw the life from a being and to command its soul while it still lived. So the people rose up and hearkened unto the vision for they believed the vision which she had given them was the true vision, and any that would not believe they called infidel.

Thus, the people learned to master the souls of the living and the dead, and they began warring against the people who worshipped the other elders; and they broke down their towers and slew their priests and recruited many to their task of finding and opening the Gate on the land.

All who would not heed them were turned against their wills by the magic of soul, and those strong enough to resist were slain and brought back by necromancy to do their master's bidding.

Then the other elders gathered together and went unto Carmen and said, "Why do such an evil thing? For, in opening the Gate, you damn us all."

But Carmen laughed and turned away from them, saying, "The Gate cannot be opened by mortal hands. My people shall slaughter your people until all turn their faces to me. And I shall be the greatest among all other gods. And when the time comes, I shall turn and slay the one whose arrow pierced my shoulder, and any who stand with her."

---

4. *Ancient,* in reference to one of the old gods, beings which existed even before the birth of the continent. Not to be confused with the *Ancient Ones,* those who lived before the time of the Great Fire.

Then Carmen departed from the presence of the other elders.

At this, the elder, Yameer, turned to the three other elders which remained with him and said, "What shall we do? And how shall we undo such a terrible thing? For there is envying in the heavens, and warring on the earth. And though Carmen believes it impossible for the people of the land to open the gate, she forgets that the people of the land once belonged to the sea and the stars, and though the land may have taken their divine gifts, true power lies in the blood; blood which now covers the land and seeps into the seas; blood with the power to wake the Ancient and open the Gate which confines him."

Then said Josadom, "Let us go unto the elder, Tai, and tell him the things which Carmen has spoken. For he is a quick and cunning elder and can outwit us all with little effort. Our predicament is a trifle thing for him to solve, and Carmen, a dispensable foe. And if he will not fight Carmen for our sake, he surely will rise up against her knowing that she seeks to harm his love."

So, the other elders hearkened unto Josadom. Thus, the elders Uulshaa, Suri Onash, Yameer, and Josadom went south unto the star upon which the elder, Tai, dwelt.

Tai stood on his balcony with Mi-Kalia, looking over his star and the people of the sky. When he saw the three elders approaching with Josadom, he said unto Mi-Kalia, "Go down and turn them away. I sense that mischief is afoot."

And when the elders came unto Tai's star, Mi-Kalia came out to greet them, saying, "What brings you here, elders who dwell among the stars?"

"Great Mother," greeted Josadom with a bow; "humbly we come to seek counsel from the Father of the Night. For a frightful thing has occurred and only he can save us."

Turning to Suri Onash, Mi-Kalia said, "Are you not a wise and just elder, Suri Onash? Surely, you can solve whatever problem is laid before you."

"Not so, Great Mother," said Suri Onash. "This problem is greater than my capabilities, therefore it demands the attention of one greater than I."

The elder, Uulshaa, was displeased by this saying, and he folded his arms before him and said, "Why has Tai sent you in his stead? Does he deem us so far below him that he will not come out to greet us himself?"

Mi-Kalia turned to Uulshaa and said, "It is not pride, but intolerance, that keeps him away. Had he come himself, you, dear brother, would surely be dead by now."

"I shall not bow before you, little sister, or address you as anything more," said Uulshaa. "We are here to see that miscreant boy. Now, let us in."

"It is true you are my older brother, Uulshaa. But in many ways, I am your superior, and you, my subordinate. And in many ways, you act the child, and I, the older of us both. Now hold your tongue, lest Tai hear you and cut it out."

Then the elders looked up and saw that Tai watched them from his balcony. And they pleaded with Mi-Kalia to let them in. But Mi-Kalia said, "Tai would not see you. Now, tell me: what is your request, that I might present it to him on your behalf?"

So the elders told Mi-Kalia all that had befallen them and all that Carmen had done.

Then said Mi-Kalia, "This is a grave and terrible thing she has done. Soon, the land will be soaked in the blood of the people, and the seal on the Gate will grow weaker still; for when our brethren descended after the Great Fire, Sor-Azarael, consumed the land, the land took from them their divine gifts because the land was too weak to hold the seal in place and needed to replenish its strength. Now it is strong, but the seal is still weak, and the Ancient, if awoken, will use the power in the blood of our brethren to release himself."

On hearing this, the elders were filled with terror and cried out saying, "We must stop Carmen."

"I agree," said Mi-Kalia. "Enter and present your case before the elder, Tai."

The elders obeyed. But Uulshaa said unto Mi-Kalia, "Will the boy not slay us if we enter uninvited?"

To this, Mi-Kalia replied, "Lo, I am with you. He shall not harm you."

So Uulshaa entered in with his sister. And when they were inside the Great Hall, they found Tai seated on his throne with his great sword, Azarael, laid across his lap. And he said with a loud voice, "What is the meaning of this intrusion? Did I not instruct you to turn them away, my love?"

Mi-Kalia stepped forward and said, "The elders have come with grave news, my love. I could not turn them away, for it pertains to us all, and you are our last hope."

Tai frowned, but said to the other elders, "Speak."

Josadom stepped forward and recounted all they had done, and all that Carmen had said and done. And when he recounted what Carmen intended to do to Mi-Kalia, Tai rose from his throne and drew his great sword from its sheath, and cut his hand upon the blade so that his blood spilled to the ground; and upon his blood and his great sword, he vowed a vow saying, "Surely, as I breathe, Carmen shall die by my blade."

But the elder, Yameer, stepped forward and said, "O Great Father of the Night, you cannot slay Carmen; for she too is an elder like us. We understand your wrath, but in your quest to protect the one you love, do you now seek to kill a god? Would you slay us all if we stood against Mi-Kalia?"

"It is not for Mi-Kalia's sake alone that I do this," said Tai. "If the seal upon the Gate is broken and the Ancient is released, then the heavens will fall alongside the land; Chaos will reign, and Leviathan will be loosed upon the seas, and the waters will run red with the blood of our people. Have you so quickly forgotten? We were given a duty alongside our divine gifts: charged to guard the Gates in the heavens and never let Chaos once again roam. That Carmen seeks to open a Gate—be it of the land, sea, or sky—shows that she is no longer with us."

Hearing this, the other elders remembered their vow to the Great Wind, Oragon, and all nodded their agreement.

To the elder, Suri Onash, Tai said, "O wise and just elder, you are yet to send a vision down to your tower and to the people who dwell upon it. Now, therefore, hear my third and final request, and heed my words: send down a vision of this treachery in the heavens, and teach the people who dwell upon your tower to know the truth, that they may see through Carmen's lies. For, as long as there are those who stand against her, there is hope." Then to all but Mi-Kalia, he said, "Once this is done, gather yourselves together, and all the people of the sky who would stand against Carmen, and you all must strengthen the heavenly

Gates. And I shall hunt and slay Carmen, and all who stand with her."

"And what of me?" asked Mi-Kalia. "Shall I remain here upon your star, cowering like a helpless creature?"

"Not so," said Tai. His voice grew soft as he approached his love and cupped her cheek in his hand. "Return to your star, and send a vision down to your people; and give them a sign that there are troubling times to come. But promise them this: that you will be with them. Thus, their hearts will be comforted in these troubling times."

So the elders departed to do as Tai had commanded, and Tai gathered all who dwelt upon his star and believed on him, and sent them with the elder, Mi-Kalia, to her star in the north. And when they arrived, she drew a sign in the heavens and sent a vision down to the people of the land. And the sign which she drew was the phoenix, shining bright in the northern sky, with the Crown of the North at its centre.

And the people perceived that troubling times lay ahead, but through it all, she would be with them; and they were greatly comforted by the vision.

And the elder, Suri Onash, painted a sign in the heavens, and the people of the land who dwelt in the North-East, beneath his star, saw the image of an owl in the stars above them. The sign was named Coba by those to the north of the mountains, and Sova by those to the south.

And for each night it shone in the sky, they that dwelt in the monolith near the Bleclif Mountains dreamed dreams and saw visions of the vow which the elders who dwelt among the stars had vowed never to let them return to the heavens; and how the elders and the ancestors of the people of the land who had descended from the stars had been tasked by the Great Wind, Oragon, to defend the gate, lest Chaos awaken; and the treachery of the elder, Carmen, who wished to use the people of the land to awaken the Ancient that slumbered.

And the people of the land who dwelt in the North-East saw these things and cried out to the elder, Suri Onash, saying; "What must we do to stop these things? For Carmen and her daemon[5] will surely destroy us all."

Then Suri Onash gave them this tenet, saying, "You must stand against the daemon, and the darkness, and the taint; for as long as there is one who stands against them, there is hope."

Thus, Suri Onash came to be known as the god of truth, for he was a wise and just elder, and had revealed the truth unto them. And the elder, Suri Onash, taught them to see and hear and know the truth, that they may never be deceived by the wicked ones; and they were them that knew a thing, and its essence thereof. And they perceived the truth and wielded the power to disperse falsehoods.

And the sign of the Great Owl Sova marked the second harvest season.

The elder, Tai, painted a sign in the stars and set a decree against Carmen and all who stood with her, saying, "Let it be known to you this day, and to those among the heavens and on the land and

---

[5]. This is the first ever reference of Carmen's followers being called *daemon*; widely translated to mean or refer to a supernatural being of a nature between gods and humans; a messenger of the gods, divinely imbued with supernatural abilities.

in the depths, that all who conspire with or grant aid to the false god, Carmen, shall henceforth be my enemy; for her sin is dire, and therefore, my vengeance shall be grave."

And the people of the land who dwelt beneath his star saw the sign and cried out to him; and Tai went forth and slew tens and thousands and tens of thousands with his great sword. And this was the sign which he drew across the heavens:

For three days, the sun did not rise; and in the South, there stood the image of the wolf with the Southern Jewel[6] as its eye; and the night sky was filled with falling stars, for there was war in the heavens, and anarchy on the land. And this sign of the wolf was called Okami, the Great Hunter.

And the people of the land who received the vision from Suri Onash carved the symbol of the owl over their doors and shrines and homes and temples, so that all who beheld it would know that they saw through all falsehoods with Sova's great eyes. And they rose up and stood against the daemon and drove them back, until all the lands of the East, from the Great Oak Tree to the southern shores, knew the truth about the things which had happened in the heavens.

The elder, Mi-Kalia, seeing the bloodshed and chaos which ravaged the land, grew grieved with Carmen, for the treacherous elder had gone and hidden herself while both the people of the land and the people who dwelt among the stars were slain for her cause. So Mi-Kalia arose and departed from her star and journeyed south to the star of the elder, Tai. And when she had

---

[6]. The star of the elder, Tai, that shone red from the blood of the people of the stars which he slew.

entered into his chambers, she found the elder, Carmen, resting in his bed.

"What is the meaning of this?" Mi-Kalia demanded, enraged by the sight.

Carmen laughed a wicked, spiteful laugh. "Did you really think you were the only one who could enter this place?" said she. "I know more ways in and out of Tai's domain than the hairs that number your head. For, once, his heart was mine, and this star was my home. It is I who should have been made great; and my name which should have been exalted. But you seduced the cunning elder and turned his heart from me, and stole all that should have been mine."

These things spake she to taunt Mi-Kalia and stir up jealousy in her heart. But Mi-Kalia said unto her, "You ignite the flames of war, then hide yourself away in your former lover's bed while people bleed and die in your name. Get up out of there and put an end to this nonsense!"

Then said Carmen, "It pleases me greatly that you, my nemesis, have presented yourself before me. Now, I will slay you and Tai's heart shall once again be mine."

To this, Mi-Kalia replied, "Have you no honour? Have you no shame? You are a liar and a coward; for you and I both know that your true ought against me is not for the sake of Tai's heart, but for access to the Gate which I protect. You wish to be rid of me so no one will stand between you and the heavenly Gate. Hate has filled your heart, and jealousy has tainted your soul. Your desire for power has been fed by the darkness from the abyss, and it has corrupted the sweet girl I once knew."

Vexed by these sayings, Carmen rose from the bed. "It is true that I desire to rule the heavens and conspire to free Chaos upon the earth. And now, I shall slay you, Mi-Kalia, for I have been strengthened by the Chief Arkon, and have been charged with this duty; and you are weak and alone and defenceless without Tai. Now, die, Mi-Kalia, and let the world be rid of your foul stench."

Then Carmen drew her axe to strike Mi-Kalia down. But Mi-Kalia took up one of Tai's swords and deflected the blow with ease.

"Foolish girl," said Mi-Kalia. "Like many others, you have taken my gentleness for weakness. You think me helpless? Let me ask you this: Would I need to bridle my heart with kindness and compassion if it were so? Would I need to temper my anger if it were not all-consuming? Would I need to stay my hand if it were weak? Would one such as Tai love me so fervently if I were nothing but a burden to him? O Carmen, you have been deceived."

Realising Mi-Kalia was neither weak nor timid, Carmen sought to deceive her by pleading for mercy. But Mi-Kalia said, "Alas, my friend. I have unburdened myself of my heart, therefore, I have no compassion to give."

So Mi-Kalia fought against Carmen and overpowered her, and bound Carmen's hands and feet with chains and brought her unto the other elders where they had gathered to protect the gate. And the elders sent word to Tai, and Tai ceased his slaughter and went unto them.

All in the heavens watched as Carmen was brought before Tai, bound with fetters of stone. And Tai said unto her, "You have done a great evil, Carmen. Repent of your sins, and send a vision down to the people who have believed on you, that they cease this needless slaughter, and perhaps I might show you mercy."

"Perhaps?" spat Carmen with her head held high. "What mercy is there for me, knowing the Crown of the North will never be mine? What sort of god would I be if I cower at your blade? I would rather burn the heavens and bathe the earth in blood. Yea, Tai, I would rather die than repent."

So Tai unshackled her and said, "I loved you once, Carmen, so I shall give you this gift: Take up your weapon and die with honour."

Then the two duelled before all the heavens, and all perceived that Tai stayed his hand against her, for he still cared for her and did not want to slay her. But Carmen was sore vexed as she battled Tai, for her pride was wounded and jealousy had consumed her heart. So she spake unto all, saying, "Even if you slay me, my daemon will not stop seeking to free the Ancient that slumbers within the earth!"

But Tai said, "We have sent a vision down to the people of the land, and we have told them the truth of the things which have occurred among the stars. The people know you are a liar, and soon, all who call upon you will repent."

Carmen laughed, saying, "Nay, my dear Tai, they will not repent. They will keep to my teachings and continue in my ways. For I am a god to them, and I have given them great power and many signs. Nothing will stop them, unless they see me fall from the stars."

Tai was grieved by her sayings, for he knew she spoke true. So he rent a hole in the heavens and pierced her heart with his great sword. Thus, the two fell from the stars in a blazing ball of fire, with Tai's great sword in Carmen's chest. And the land split in two where Carmen's back struck the Garua, and the bridge crumbled; but the foundations of the bridge were made of whitestone, and it held the west to the rest of the land.

All who dwelt near the Garua saw Carmen fall from the stars, and fear gripped their hearts and they repented, saying, "How has the great god of the Garua fallen? And what great sin could one commit to be cast down from the heavens?"

But, on hearing this, Carmen laughed a laugh, and with her blood and her dying breath, she sealed the sign of the Archer in the stars, that the people who still believed on her would forever look upon it and be reminded of their duty.

Thus, the elder, Carmen, was slain by Tai's great sword. And her blood seeped into the land. And the seal on the Gate beneath the land weakened further because of the great quake from the fall of the gods and the blood of Carmen. And one among them that were sealed with the Ancient who slumbered was freed to roam the land. And it fled from Tai's presence and hid itself in shadows so that the elder would not find it.

Thus, Tai sent a message to the elders who dwelt among the stars, saying, "Carmen is dead. Now, find one who is worthy to stand in her stead, and appoint them to fulfil her duties. I shall remain on the land; and I shall hunt the Arkon who wraps itself in shadows and darkness. For the seal has been weakened further, and there is none else who can defend it."

Mi-Kalia knew Tai would be grieved to have slain Carmen and burdened with finding the Arkon, and she sought to come unto him, but Tai refused her, saying, "Keep watch in the heavens, and stand guard over the Gates, that none rise up in Carmen's place and wreak havoc among the stars. And once this is ended, I will come unto you, and we will never be parted again."

Then with his great sword, he sliced his hand, and with his blood, he drew a blanket in the skies over the sign of the Archer. And the covering was to last six hundred and sixty six years before the evil sign was to be revealed and he would need to cast a new covering once more.

So Tai hunted the Arkon who had been set free on the land, and he appointed one from among the people of the land to hunt and slay the daemon and all who sought to free the Ancient who slumbered within the earth. And in the heavens, the elders appointed one named Duriel to rule in Carmen's stead; for Duriel was loyal to Tai and was like a son to Mi-Kalia.

He it was who was the first born of the Fallen. The elder, Mi-Kalia, took him from his cot on the night he was born, for he was conceived in the stars and thus did not lose the gifts given to the people who dwelt among the stars by the Great Wind, Oragon; So the elder, Mi-Kalia, would that he did not suffer the same fate as the Fallen, for he transgressed not.

And those who believed upon Carmen were exceedingly wrought that she be called the Fallen God, and that she was slain by the Elder, Tai. And so they took the moniker and named Tai the Fallen God, and spun tales of his bloodshed in the heavens and how he was cast down from the stars for his transgression. This they did so all whom he wished to appoint to slay them would be turned away from him and none would do his bidding. But there were those upon the land who knew the truth and worshipped at the altar of the Warrior God, and they were still willing to do his bidding.

As the great wind returned me to the Field of Kesindrath, I lay on the bed of blue melonia flowers and wept with grief for the things I had seen: for the selfishness of the elders; and the wickedness of Carmen; and the sacrifice of Tai.

Then she approached me once more and asked, "Do you understand the vision?"

With a heavy heart, I replied, "No, I do not. This is a terrible tale, and I fear it holds little meaning to me, save stirring up in my heart a distrust for the gods; for their skirmish in the heavens, men do bleed."

"The vision is of things which have already come to pass," said she. "It is of a time long forgotten and a truth often mistold. For the people of the land remember not the evils Carmen wrought, and perceive not that the sign in the sky which she sealed with her blood is one that will lead to destruction."

I cast my eyes to the heavens, and lo, the Archer stood in the sky, his arrow aimed at the Crown of the North, as though wishing to strike it down. And I perceived that this was the vision I had seen; for, in her jealousy, the elder, Carmen, had sought to strike down the Great Mother.

As I lay among the blue melonia flowers, watching the heavens, I listened, and again I heard the faint whisper of a promise: *It is well. I am with you. I will always be with you.* But my soul remained troubled by the things I had seen, and my heart would not be comforted by these words.

APOSTACY

Rising from the bed of blue melonias, I turned to her and bowed low.

"Have you purposed in your heart to forsake the path of truth?" asked she.

Then spake I unto her, saying, "Why should truth shroud itself in darkness and understanding hide from plain sight? With each vision, my heart grows troubled, yet my mind is unfruitful; and I comprehend neither the sayings of the gods nor the visions of mortal men. It is not the truth I forsake, Ancient One[1], but this path of confusion and lies."

I turned to take my leave, but as I started away from the field, she rose and came after me, saying, "Patience, my child. In time, understanding will come."

"O Goddess," said I, "I am but a mortal; a blade of grass in a great field; one which withers in the heat of the sun and perishes with no bearing on the field in which it sprouted. I am here today, and gone tomorrow, and when tomorrow comes, another will take my place. Wait for him, goddess, and to him

---

1. Here, Schandrof makes a distinction between the *Ancients* and the *Ancient Ones*, the latter often referring to those who lived before the time of the Great Fire.

show these visions, that perhaps he might perceive them with an understanding heart and do your bidding."

As I departed from the field, she watched me, her expression sullen and her eyes glistening with tears. It was a grave thing to defy a goddess, to break the heart of one so great and lovely and pure. But my mind was in turmoil from the visions, and I feared to witness anymore, lest madness be my portion.

Can one hide from the gods? I shall surely try, peradventure sleep shall elude me no more. For I am a man of simple means; desiring little and wanting nothing more than a roof over my head, food on my table, and clothes on my back. I have asked for naught more than what I need to survive. I have taken only what has been freely given.

Why then do these visions still trouble me? Why does the face of the goddess haunt me every time I close my eyes? Is it not right that I choose my own destiny? Is it not right that I follow in my father's footsteps and lead a peaceful life?

I am but a moon shy of manhood[2]; with a trade and a woman to soon call my own. Shall I forsake such a promising future for madness? Shall I cast this aside for an insanity inflicted by the hand of a god?

Not so.

I shall choose my own destiny.

The lovely Fiadh is finally mine. She whispers softly in my ear, confessing her love. It fills my heart to bursting. Now, we shall begin a new life—away from her home and the father undeserving of a daughter so kind. She worries that I might find her hideous for her wounds, but the scars only make her more beautiful in my eyes.

For the pain she has felt, I shall give her joy threefold, and we shall build a happy home, with plenty of laughter and a half a dozen children. For the rest of my days, I shall wake to her beautiful smile; to a beauty which outshines that of the goddess herself. My Fiadh; my love.

It has been a moon since my Fiadh and I were wed. Children still do not come, though I perceive that they will not for a time.

This troubles my Fiadh. She fears it is her fault. I do not concur, for this will only worsen her condition. The physician has assured me that she only need rest; her body still heals from the suffering inflicted upon it.

I wish to kill her father. I wish to end the man that still causes her to weep at night (she does this in secret when she thinks I am asleep). I close my eyes and strangle him in my dreams; but his death will not heal my Fiadh's pain. So I hold her close and whisper to her that I love her, and I always will, whether we have threescore children or none.

The winter cold enters Fiadh's bones. She protests that I would not let her trade at the market. She is used to hard labour and feels lost with nothing to do.

I will not relent on my stance.

Though she tries to hide it, I can see the stiffness in her movements; I can tell there's an ache in her broken leg. She does not complain, or ask for more than she is given—I give her a lot more than she could want or need.

Fiadh no longer speaks of children; I do not bring it up. I know it is a thorn in her flesh and I do not wish to prod it. But I cannot let my Fiadh continue to suffer.

I have sold the farm for a small fortune. It is enough to afford a new life in the capital, and proper treatment for my Fiadh.

I have secured for myself an old smithy, and for Fiadh, an apprenticeship at the temple: she will not be pleased I keep her confined and unproductive. Mother Yrnanon, at the temple of the Great Mother, has assured me that her tasks will be restricted to the archives, where her greatest strain will be shelving tomes.

If this is not considered a worthy compromise, then none else will.

Trouble stirs among the people; whispers of war fill the street. Though the empire prospers under the mighty hand of Emperor Vladicsar, all is not as it seems.

I sense a stirring in the heavens. Something slithers in the darkness, though we perceive it not.

I look up and behold, in the sky, there is a sign: it is the Archer who points his arrow to the Crown of the North. My heart is troubled once more. I know this sign to be that of the evil elder, Carmen; for it was shown to me in the visions which I did not understand.

It is the sign of the one which stirs up darkness in the hearts of men and persuades them to do evil.

There is a stirring in the heavens; something foul slithers in the darkest depths of the earth.

War looms on the horizon; the people of the forest gather: sorcerers and warriors. Rebels. They build an army and seek to depose the emperor.

All able-bodied men who have worked the fields and seen a dozen and four moons[3] have been called upon to take up arms and defend the empire against such traitors. I, too, shall fight for my people; for my home; for the wife of my youth and the child in her womb; for I have now seen a score moons[4] grace the heavens.

---

3. Sixteen years

4. Twenty years

I too shall take up arms against these rebels, and I shall defend my home.

The training is harsh, the planes are inhospitable outside the city walls. A famine; a curse cast upon the empire by the people of the forest. Winter fast approaches and General Manon assures us that conditions will only worsen.

Game is scarce. The water grows toxic, and soon it will be undrinkable. We live on rations, train our bodies with harsh exercises, and fend off fell creatures; animals morphed by the curse and the taint.

Our party travels south, drawing closer to the place I once called home. Even without seeing it, I know the old farm which was once mine is now ravaged and desolate. Yet, the forest stands tall and evergreen, secure in the shadow of the Sacred Mountain; undefiled by this foul sorcery that the people have loosed upon our world.

Each night, she calls to me. I hear her voice in my ear, like the sound of a babbling brook, saying, "Rise, my child; come to me."

Night after night, she calls to me, wearing down my soul even as war creeps closer still. So I shall answer. I shall go to the field where we first met, and I shall beg her to leave me be, for my wife is heavy with child and I am soon to go off to battle.

I fear that my child shall grow up without a father, and my wife shall have none to comfort her. I am not a man of war. I am untrained in the art of combat, and I fear I will not survive the coming battle.

Therefore, now, let me go to her, peradventure, she might look favourably on me and preserve my life. I shall go to the meadows and search for the blue melonia flower until I find the field of the gods, that I might commune with one once more.

PART TWO
THE PRESENT WHICH IS STILL BEING WRITTEN

THE PRESENT WHICH IS STILL BEING WRITTEN

I have journeyed to Kesindrath, to the field of blue melonia flowers, and here I shall lay down to rest. My eyelids grow laden with sleep as I breathe in the gold pollen that hovers about me like a cloud. Surely, she will come to me. Surely, she will not forsake me in my time of need. Surely as the sun shall rise, she will find me in the place where we first met.

She came from the skies, as though descending invisible stairs. I rose to meet her. Draped in a flowing gown of white, threads of silver were laced about her curled ivory horns and hung over her face, holding stars in her braided golden hair; gold dust sparkled on her bronzen skin, and her eyes burned with a fierceness that drove me to my knees.

"My goddess," whispered I, my face pressed to the earth.

There was no gentleness in her voice as she said, "You call me goddess, yet when I speak, you do not listen; when I call, you do not answer; when I instruct, you do not obey."

"Forgive me, goddess," I pleaded. "I am but a man: foolish and unbridled and given to follow the lusts and desires of my heart. The things which you once showed me drove me to the brink of madness; yet now I perceive some meaning from them. I have seen the sign of the Archer in the sky; I have felt the stirring in the heavens and the slitherings deep within the earth. And I perceive that the things which I saw written in the past are soon to repeat themselves: for war comes from the west and rebels gather in the forest to overthrow the emperor."

Then said she, "Rise, my child. It is as you perceive it to be; yet it is not. Two and two things have I shown you: things of the past which cannot be unwritten. Now, therefore, tarry with me a while, and I shall show you three visions; of the present which is still being written. Then shall you perceive the truth of that which slithers beneath the earth and understand the meaning of the stirrings in the heavens and the sign in the stars and the warring in the west and the people of the forest."

Climbing to my feet before her, I stood a head taller than the tips of her horns. Even so, I felt small in her presence. Small as a grain of pollen in this field of flowers.

Taking my hand in hers, she spake unto me, saying, "Come, my child. Let me show you that which pertains to things which are still being written."

At her words, I was swept up by a great wind and taken to a field of stars in a deep blue sky, and here, I was shown things which are still being written.

THE FIFTH VISION

I looked down over the land and beheld its many wonders: the tower of Murah and the Garua to the West; the Old Oak Tree to the East; and Siren's Bay[1] to the south. The people waxed great, and the empire was strong under the mighty hand of the Great Emperor, Vladicsar, for the emperor wielded magic with great proficiency though he curtailed the use of it for the safety of those who did not possess the power to wield it; and his palace was great, and all who dwelt in it rejoiced.

As I looked upon the palace, I saw a boy climb over the wall and into the emperor's inner courtyard. I perceived he was a few moons shy of manhood—barely five moons younger than I—and in his arms, he bore a book. When he reached the door to the emperor's chambers, he knocked once, then twice, then once more. I waited for a time, as did he. When finally the door opened, I beheld the emperor, Vladicsar, in a flowing blue robe

---

1. Also known as the Broken Lands and, in more recent times, the Isles. It is believed that the Isles were broken off from the mainland by the intervention of a goddess who came from the sea to save the descendants of those who had ascended to the surface after the Great Fire, Sor-Azarael, destroyed the land.

of fine silk. His auburn hair fell over one shoulder, and sleep clung to his eyelids.

I started, for never before had I seen the emperor alone and so simply dressed. Without his armour and golden crown, he looked much younger than I had imagined him to be.

On seeing the boy, the emperor immediately grew alert. "It is late, Adrien," said the emperor. "You should be asleep."

The boy presented the book to the emperor who stared down at it with mild irritation.

Perceiving that this was no ordinary book, I strained to see it. As I did, I was drawn down to the land, and my feet were placed upon the palace steps. And though I stood in their midst, neither the emperor nor the boy could see me.

The emperor glanced this way and that before opening the door wide to admit the boy. He shuffled in and I entered behind him. The emperor's chamber was opulent, with gold-leafed furnishings of lacquered black wood. Curtains of reds and golds hung over the windows and the canopy of his bed which was covered in cushions and quilts.

Ignoring the cushions arranged on the floor in the seating area, Adrien climbed into the emperor's bed and folded his legs beneath him. When the emperor came to sit opposite him, Adrien placed the book on the bed between them and said, "I have studied the writings contained within this book. It is true that this path will give you unrivalled strength, but it comes at great cost."

"What cost is too great for the ruler of the world?" said the emperor with a laugh. "Name the price, and I shall pay it with ease."

But the boy shook his head. "It is not one you can pay with ease; for this power comes at the cost of your very soul."

At this, the emperor frowned. "How so?"

"It is a foul teaching," said Adrien; "One built on lies from a false god. The signs are true, I agree. But the power shall corrupt your heart, and though you may wax great, you will lose yourself. You will no longer be you."

"Would you rather I let my people perish at the hands of those who seek to free magic?" said the emperor. "Would you rather they died of a plague induced by sorcery? The rebels grow too bold, Rien. They trade enchantments in the shadows and transform themselves into beasts of prey. Should I do nothing as they hide out in the forest and amass an army in the shadow of the Sacred Mountain? Soon, they will seek to overthrow me."

Adrien bowed his head, and his voice was a broken whisper as he asked, "Have you not suffered enough? Have *we* not sacrificed enough for the people?" A tear ran down his cheek. "Each day, I feel you slipping further and further away. I watch you pour out your heart and soul for a people who will never love you as much as I do. To them, you are replaceable; to me, you are not."

The boy began to weep, and the emperor pulled him into his arms and cradled his head to his chest. "There, there," said the emperor. "You know I am the emperor, Adrien. I have a duty to the empire."

"Before you were the emperor, you were first my father," said Adrien.

The revelation shocked me to my core, for none in the empire knew that Emperor Vladicsar had a son.

"I was—and still am—your father, Rien," said the emperor. "And one day, this empire shall be yours. But you must be mindful that you are sixteen now, and a man in the eyes of the people. What would others think if you were discovered sneaking into my bedchamber at night?"

At this, the boy hugged the emperor tighter and wept even more, and I perceived that it was because he could not see his father whenever he pleased.

"The ministers have spoken, Rien," said the emperor. "I must listen; lest I be called a tyrant."

Adrien wept in his father's arms until finally, he fell asleep. As I watched, the emperor rose from the bed and, picking up the book, sat on the floor at the foot of the bed and began to read. And as he read, I saw darkness like a mist come up from the book. It surrounded the emperor and sought a way to enter into his heart, but it found none, so it returned into the pages of the book.

Then I was caught up by a great wind and lifted far up into the sky; And I saw the Sacred Mountain below. People gathered within the forest beside it; children played in clearings around hearths or slept in tents. And as I watched, men and women changed into beasts of prey and hunted for food. And men and women lived within the trees of the forest and called it their home.

These people were a peaceful folk, content with life and happy to be left alone, not rebels and traitors amassing an army as the emperor and the empire had been led to believe.

And I questioned this in my heart, saying, "Who has deceived us so?"

Then I heard the voice of the Great Mother carried on the wind, and she said, "Look."

I looked, and behold, I saw the Council Hall. And gathered within it was the Trade Council. In the hall, I saw a darkness like that which had risen from the book which the emperor read. It permeated the entire hall, coating it in shadow as it swirled and writhed around the ministers, entering into their souls through their noses and ears and mouths.

And the ministers spake to one another, saying, "Come, now, what are we to do with such infidels? If the emperor himself will not turn, then we must act, and we must cut them down before they increase in number."

Then said the minister who sat at the head of the table, "Calm yourselves, brethren. The emperor will surely turn; for there is none who reads the Book of Souls whose heart is not stirred towards the Great Goddess and her cause."

And I perceived in my heart that the wicked elder, Carmen, was the one of whom he spoke; for, as they rose in agreement to conclude their meeting, the minister who stood at the head said, "The Chief Arkon shall rise again."

And to that, the others responded, "And we along with him."

The great wind returned me to the bed of blue melonias, and I said in my heart that returning was a grave mistake; for I found this vision to be more troubling than the tempest and confusing as a desert storm.

Turning to the goddess, I said, "What shall I make of these things which you have shown me? The emperor's heart is pure, but the Council has been corrupted by darkness. Thus, they have fed the emperor lies and made him believe that they who dwell in the forest by the Sacred Mountain are traitors and rebels; but these are a peaceful people, though they possess the power to transform into beasts."

But she sat beside me, and folded her legs beneath her and said, "The vision is of things which are. The vision may be unclear now, but with time, understanding shall come. You only need listen."

"Nay," said I. "I have listened with my heart, yet understanding has eluded me with each vision, though my soul remains troubled by the things which I see. Now, I shall see them no more; for I came in search of aid, that peradventure, I might survive the war which is to come, but all I have found is madness and more shadowy tales that steer my heart towards sorrow."

I rose from the bed of blue melonias, leaving her sitting in the field of flowers, and this time, she did not come after me.

TEMPEST OF SOULS

Our training grows even more rigorous as the days go by. General Manon says the emperor is hesitant to go to war. He would that this conflict be solved amicably, for no matter the victor, it is the empire that will suffer the calamities of war. He has sent emissaries into the forest; many do not return.

The Trade Council tries increasingly to persuade the emperor to battle. They spout lies in his ears and sow evil plans in his heart. I know this scheme is one orchestrated by the ministers. I know the emissaries are false; men planted by the Council and willing to end their own lives if only to further their cause.

But I have no proof of this, so I hold my tongue. I have a family to protect. My wife is heavy with child, and it is my duty to keep them safe.

They emerged from the forest in the dead of night. They attacked our camp and wounded our patrols.

The general is furious. But I find it odd that they took no lives though they had the chance. The injured are to return to the city; new men recruited to replenish our numbers. I am to return to the city with them, for a missive came for me at dawn, carrying grave news: I am no longer to be a father.

General Manon has granted me leave, for I must return to be with my Fiadh.

I find comfort in Fiadh's arms. I hope I provide her with the same measure of peace. It has been a season since I returned unto her. She has requested that we celebrate the life almost had, rather than mourn the one lost.

She is stronger now. Her smiles have become more frequent, even as my heart breaks each day, for I know I must return to the battlefield; to the looming war before the forest. I remind her of this each night as we lay in each other's arms. Each night, she pleads with me to remain, to maim myself if I must. She does not want to lose me.

I cannot stay. I know the truth: of the sign in the heavens and the ones which stir up conflict in the empire, though I have no proof.

I must return to the field of battle. I know not why, only that that is my place.

General Manon is relieved by my return. He says I am either brave or foolish. I wager the latter. Either way, my loyalty has been rewarded with a promotion, and I am now given charge over the new recruits. I must train them to be strong, teach them to be brave.

My comrades cheer, but I do not. For I am charged with teaching children to neglect their own safety and throw their lives away for a foolish cause at the behest of evil men who dwell safely in their homes. I am charged to murder; to snuff out these promising new flames before they have the chance to truly burn. I am charged to become a monster.

A missive came unto the General at dawn. My Fiadh is with child once more. Why does my heart grow troubled by this great and joyous news?

I have met the one called Adrien. He has been placed under my command. He is a sweet boy: slow to anger and quick to forgive all who have wronged him. He perceives not that I know whose seed he is.

Many a night, he has snuck out of camp and into his father's tent. He does not know that I am the reason he has not been caught: I secretly distract the guards to grant him safe passage.

I know he tries to dissuade his father from war. He speaks freely of his desire for peace and professes his belief that no rebels lurk in the forest. I wish to tell him that he is right, but that would mean confessing to him the things I know. And though he is a kind boy, he is vocal with his beliefs and would surely bring trouble to my doorstep, should he know the truth.

The Ministers grow desperate. Their emissaries attacked our camp under the guise of the forest people. Their weapons give them away: they are too finely crafted to belong to the people of the forest.

Tonight, we shall hold a burning for the fallen recruits.

The General offers words of comfort. It is not sorrow that fills me, but rage. I know the reason for this strike. I know it is because Adrien is among us. They seek to force the emperor's hand. Their ploy has worked. Word has already reached us that the emperor is furious. There are whispers that he intends to march on the people of the forest, to eradicate them; he will burn the entire forest down if he must.

Adrien grows weary of training. He is lax in his duties, and even his visits to his father have become infrequent. I can only conclude that he is disenchanted with his purpose to end the war before it begins.

Joyous word has reached my ears: My wife has borne me a son. She worries that I am at the front, that I have so quickly advanced in rank. She fears what will become of Brendan if I do not return.

I have sent word assuring her that I will indeed return unto her. I will live to raise our little Brendan.

The men worry for Adrien. He does not eat or sleep, and the fat flees from off his bones. He grows pale and gaunt with each passing day. His soul wanes, and his heart grows weak. I see the sorrow in his eyes.

Many under my command have come to me in secret to share their worry for him: they fear he will not see the next moon. They would that I speak with him, but there is little I can say to heal his heart, for it is obvious that it is broken.

It has been three days since Adrien last left his tent.

His condition worsens far more than I imagined. Now, I shall go and speak with him and discover what it is that hurts his soul so. Perhaps, in doing so, I might find a way to heal the guilt that gnaws at mine.

The boy is frail with sickness. He barely speaks, and movement is agony for him. I perceive it is a sickness not of this world. I have sent word to his father in secret, but he will not come, lest he expose his son prematurely and put him in further danger.

The emperor raves in his chambers. His stewards report that he is racked with sorrow and madness, but none know the cause. I know it is for Adrien's sake he is distraught; I, too, am a father, and though I have not met my little Brendan, I worry about him greatly.

I shall sit with Adrien and watch over him tonight. For, were my Brendan in Adrien's place and I could not come unto him, I would that he be with someone he can trust. Come dawn, I shall send Adrien home.

We spoke at length, Adrien and I.

He knows of the darkness that slithers beneath the earth. He, too, has seen the visions of the things which cannot be unwritten, and he perceives that the daemon are responsible for his condition. The Council blames the people of the forest for the blight which they have caused; they seek to force the emperor's hand.

Adrien tells me that the blight which afflicts him is the same that was cast by the daemon upon the ones they call infidels in order to control their souls; for it is a curse which has its directions written in the Book of Souls by the instruction of an elder who dwelt among the stars. It is necromancy.

I know this to be true, because the goddess showed me the visions and I saw Adrien read the book. He speaks freely to me. He fears his end is nigh and would that the truth be known. He laments the thought of being considered mad with fever, he does not realise that I, too, have seen the visions and know the things which he says to be true.

My heart is heavy with guilt. I consider sharing with him the things which I have seen. I would not that he died thinking himself to be alone and mad. The next time we speak, I shall tell him the truth.

Adrien does not wake. His breathing is shallow and broken. Yet, he whispers in his sleep; he wishes to be taken to the people of the forest[1]. To the one called Bartolome Telk.

I believe this Bartolome Telk holds answers to questions we have not yet considered to ask.

Perhaps he knows of a way to heal Adrien. Despite the blight, the Sacred Forest remains healthy, and the people within are untouched by the blight. Perhaps they can save Adrien.

I grow desperate. His condition worsens and there is no remedy for this blight. But if there is a chance, then I must take it. I would not that he die on my watch. I know too well the pain of losing a child. I, too, am a father. I would not that another man's son should die for my inaction.

We will enter the Sacred Forest and save Adrien, or perish alongside him.

The people of the forest are not rebels. They know the empire's armies surround them, yet they take up no arms to fight.

They welcomed us when I and my small band of trusted men arrived bearing Adrien on a cot.

Bartolome Telk says it was wise to have brought him when we did, for the darkness would have stripped his soul from his body,

---

1. It is believed, from this account, that the Rebels dwelt in the village of Nytefall, in the Peney Forest, north of the Sacred mountain.

given a few suns more. He is a muradora, a healer schooled in the arts of magic. He will treat Adrien, though he warns that the curse of this blight will surely leave its mark on the boy.

Three days have passed since we brought Adrien to the forest. He is awake now. He speaks and sits and eats on his own, though walking still tires him. When we are alone, we speak of the secrets we shared on his deathbed. I confess the truth: he is not mad, for I, too, have been shown these visions by the goddess.

Adrien urges me to return to the goddess once more. He believes she will show me a way to end the war, for it was one which began in the heavens many lifetimes ago.

I do not wish to return. I do not wish to be shown visions I do not understand. Instead, I shall go to the emperor and reveal to him the things of the past and the things which are still being written. I know he is a wise and just man, and he will surely listen to reason.

The emperor has gone mad.

He believes his son dead, his body stolen by the rebels who poisoned him with a magical plague. He believes they seek to destroy his empire and seize his sceptre.

He hears my words but does not perceive their meaning. He desires to find the rebel leader; he desires the power to awaken the dead and bring his son back to life. He does not believe that Adrien is alive and well.

I perceive he has been bewitched by some foul sorcery, and in his grief, has succumbed to insanity. I fear there may be no way to save him.

This news has weakened Adrien's heart. He pleads with me night and day to return to the goddess and beseech her help. I have commanded him to cease his requesting; he has become like a son to me, and I feel my resolve giving way under the pressure, for I do not wish to trouble his frail heart any further.

I returned to the Field of Kesindrath, where the blue melonia flowers had once blossomed; where the goddess had twice met me and shown me such troubling visions.

The blue melonias do not bloom. The goddess does not hearken to my call.

Adrien would that I return each night until she does. I have neither the spirit nor the will for such a feat. I worry for my wife and son. None have seen or heard from them since I was named the rebel leader and branded a traitor to the empire.

It was the Council's doing; for my conversation with the emperor was surely relayed to them, and they realised I have seen the truth. They pressure the emperor to move upon the people of the forest, but the part of the man that once feared the gods and did good still resists their evil ways.

The emperor received the letter signed by Adrien's hand, and it has calmed his spirit. He has responded in kind to his son, and

Adrien tells me that the emperor wishes to be rid of the Book of Souls, but the darkness from the book still fights relentlessly to possess him; and he fears he cannot win.

He beseeches me in his letter to seek the goddess once more, that peradventure, she will come down and save a dying empire from the darkness that seeks to consume it.

The emperor has sent my Fiadh and Brendan unto me, delivered safely and in secret by General Manon, along with a note of thanks. After learning what lengths I went to to save Adrien, he took it upon himself to save my family. Now, we are made even.

The emperor has sent the General with three bags of silver coins, five vats of oil, three bags of flour, two drums of wine, threescore sharpened weapons, and ten trusted men to fight by my side. He beseeches me to once more seek the goddess and beseech her aid before the empire falls into darkness.

I have become that which they perceived me to be. "King of the Forest" they cry as I lead men to defend the borders; as I return with few, the fallen numbering greater with each skirmish. Like a prophecy unfitly spoken, that which was once a curse upon my name has become the truth of my existence. Shall I truly lead a people to freedom? Do they think me wise enough? Fierce enough?

Nay.

It is foolishness, and not wisdom, that is the reason for my appointment. These people believe me to be a man madder than the emperor himself—one mad enough to challenge him and risk his life to defend them. They forget that I, too, am a man just as they; I, too, have a family I do not wish to be separated from.

I, too, fear the flames of war that now ravage the lands and the desolation that will surely be left behind when the ash finally settles.

Three hundred and seventy days have passed since the Pearl of Pyxis last blessed us with her light; since I last sought the goddess in an empty field. Though the enemy marches, we shall not be discouraged. We believe she shall return to us, that great and glorious goddess, our light and hope, our lady of the night. We shall not be discouraged, but wait, we shall, until she turns her face to us once more.

The blue melonias have blossomed once more. Little Brendan brought a single flower from the side of the Sacred Mountain. Adrien believes it to be a sign that the goddess has smiled upon us.

Might I once again converse with the Ancient One with bronzen skin and curled ivory horns? Might I again see visions of things which I do not understand?

The emperor has gone mad once more, his moments of lucidness fewer and far-between. Even as he advances his army upon the people of the forest, he writes to his son requesting that I seek the goddess.

We are in the midst of war, with men, women and children falling on either side. My people look to me for guidance. My enemy looks to me for aid. It is too great a burden for any one man to bear.

Now, therefore, let me seek out the field of god-flowers, that perchance, I might breathe in that fog of gold and be graced with the goddess's guidance.

RETURN

She came from nowhere. Her feet made no sound upon the field, neither did the train of her flowing white gown whisper as she approached where I sat upon an outcropping at the side of the Sacred Mountain. Her golden hair and bronzen skin shimmered in the moonlight, and on her head, she wore a laurel of ivy and thorns.

I fell on my face in reverence.

She did not speak as she approached, and though I could not see her face, I knew she looked upon me with contempt.

"Forgive me once more, Great Goddess," I pleaded. "I have seen the error of my ways. I am branded a traitor, considered an outcast by my people, and my emperor wrestles with the darkness from the Book of Souls. The daemon rise again, for the Archer shines bright in the night sky. Soon, they will poison the land with their taint, and all who do not bend to the will of the False God will fall."

"What has this to do with me?" asked she.

Straightening on my knees to look up at her, I said, "I come not just for my sake, but for the sake of all who have believed on your name. Both my comrades and my foes look to me for answers I do not have. Answers which lie with you. This is a war that began in the heavens, and now we, the people of the land, do bear the brunt of its wrath. Therefore, Great Goddess, shew me what I must do and guide my hand aright, lest we perish by the will of a vengeful elder long since dead."

She considered this a while before finally saying, "I shall grant your request on the condition that you remain to witness all I have to show you. If you do not, if you should leave once more without witnessing the visions, the people of the forest will perish, and all that you love will be burned with fire; and no matter how you seek me, you will not find me; no matter how you call on me, I will not answer."

This saying filled my heart with fear, and I trembled at her words. But I remembered the pleas of Adrien and the emperor; the smile of my wife and the laugh of my son. And for them, I strengthened my resolve and said, "I have heard your warning, and I shall heed it. I do not intend to depart without a way to lighten the burden which rests heavy on my shoulders. Now, Goddess, show me that which I am to see; tell me that which I am to know."

"For two moons you have sought me. Two and two things I shall now show you: things of the present, and things which have not yet come to pass."

At her words, I was swept up by a great wind and taken to a field of stars in a deep blue sky, and here, I was shown the things which are still being written.

THE SIXTH VISION

I looked down from the heavens and I saw a dark fog rising from the Council Hall. It crept over the land, and all in its path were tainted by it. And I saw the Council gather together; and he who sat at the head of the table rose to welcome the emperor into their midst.

All stood in greeting as Emperor Vladicsar entered the room. Darkness shrouded him, the evil fog flowing in and out of him like it did the members of the Council. I was filled with horror at the sight; the emperor I loved and served was but a husk of the young and vibrant man I had last seen. Even in all his madness, he had never looked so emaciated.

The emperor walked stiffly; every so often, his lips twitched and his eyes looked this way and that, as though he searched the hall for something none else could see. In his left hand, he carried the Book of Souls, and he clutched his right hand tightly to his chest. When he took his seat at the head of the table, he placed the book before him. It was only when he rested his right hand on the table that I perceived a small object was hid within it.

I strained to see what it was, and as I did, I was drawn into the room and my feet were placed firmly on the floor of the council room, beside where the emperor sat. And I realised that the thing which he had clutched so tightly to his heart was a gold locket on a chain. I recognised the necklace instantly, for Adrien wore its twin.

The council member who sat at the other head of the table and had risen to welcome the emperor spoke with a loud voice and said, "We have all seen the sign in the heavens; how the Archer burns bright in the night sky. The time is come to squash the rebels in the forest. It is time we rid this world of the infidels. And no greater hand exists that can bring salvation to our world than that of the Great Emperor Vladicsar himself!" He gestured to the emperor, and all cheered.

But the emperor did not smile in response; for there was a warring within him. And through his eyes, I glimpsed that there still existed a shard of his soul. My heart was greatly troubled to watch that sliver of being that was the true emperor fight for control of his body; to watch it squeeze the locket on the table and draw strength from it.

"Fight!" I urged, though I knew he could not hear me. "You must fight!"

With all my strength, I willed the emperor to return to the man he had once been. The people of the forest were skilled healers, and being worshippers of the Great Mother and the Great Owl, they possessed the strength to drive back the darkness from the soul. If only the emperor could fight long enough to be brought unto them, then there was a chance he could be saved, though I doubted he would ever be the great and glorious man that he once was. For I had learned that every curse leaves a mark, and even Adrien, though recovered, would always remain frail and sickly after his soul had been touched by such dark magic.

The Council was silent, waiting expectantly for the emperor to address them. On noticing the emperor's struggle, they began a chant; a foul-sounding thing in a language I could not understand.

Then the emperor began to tremble, and as I watched, I saw the fog of black grow thick and envelop him, sliding up his nose and down his throat, filling him and drowning his soul in darkness. I watched the spark of soul flounder in the fog, desperately seeking salvation.

Instinctively, I reached for him.

I gasped when my hand closed about his, solid as steel between my fingers. The remnants of the soul that was my emperor looked at me, and I knew in my heart that he could truly see me.

"Schandrof," whispered he, clasping my forearm, even as his slipped in my grasp. Tears ran down his cheeks, and I felt mine grow wet as his strength faded. "Save my empire," he said. "Save my son."

Nodding once, I saw hope glimmer in his teary eyes. As I sought to pull him out from the abyss, darkness slithered up to embrace the emperor and sought to drag him down into its depths. But I would not relent, for there was still hope.

Seeing my struggle, the emperor smiled at me—warm and tender as a father would his beloved child. "Protect my Adrien, Schandrof," he said. "Watch over my son."

Then the emperor let go.

My heart shattered within me as the great Emperor Vladicsar—the man I revered and adored and had sworn to serve with my life—slipped from my grasp.

I could do nothing as the darkness swallowed him whole.

The great wind returned me to the Sacred Mountain, and there I fell to my knees and wept. My heart was filled with deep sorrow, for my emperor was no more. Furthermore, I feared what would become of Adrien should he learn of his father's fate.

Turning my face to the goddess, I cried, "What sort of thing is this? Is it not enough that I be burdened with the cares of my family and the people of the forest? Now, the emperor has thrust upon me a greater obligation to his empire and to his son."

"It is no greater a burden than that which you already bear, my child. Adrien is your son in all but blood, and you, his father. Furthermore, the burden for the people is one you have always carried in your heart. That is why you sought me out as a child; it is why I answered, and why I chose to show you the visions. It is why you once returned to me in search of the strength to fight this war, and why you return to me now seeking the path to end it. The Father of the Night has chosen you from among your kin to be a saviour of your world."

Perplexed by her words, I asked, "What do you mean? I have neither met the great elder, Tai, nor has he spoken to me in times past. Why then do you say that he has chosen me to be a saviour?"

"Come, my child," said she. "It is a thing which pertains to the final vision of that which is still being written. Now, therefore, dry your eyes and steady your heart; that which I shall show you is grave and fearful."

At her words, I was swept up by a great wind, and was taken across the empire, to where the land split during the Great Fall.

And there, I was shown the final vision of the things which are still being written.

THE SEVENTH VISION

I stood upon the foundations of the Garua, and there approached me a man with hair of the fairest gold and eyes as red as blood; and with him was one with a crown of stars on his head and an earring which shone like the moon.

With them was one with galaxies in his eyes; and he it was who held a great sword in his hand.

And I saw that the hilt of the sword was carved from whitestone, and its blade was forged from black diamond, and he had imbued it with the mana of the gods, for he was the Ancient One who had dwelt upon the Southern Jewel and caused the heavens to tremble at the mention of his name.

Perceiving that this was the elder, Tai, who approached me, I fell on my face in reverence.

"Rise, child," said he.

My heart trembled with fear at the sound of his voice.

When I did not move, he said, "Rise, great warrior."

Slowly, I lifted my head and said, "Forgive me, mighty elder of the skies; I am no great warrior."

Ignoring my words, the elder turned and they that were with him did the same. I perceived that they wanted me to follow, so I rose and went after them.

At the edge of the Garua, a chasm yawned open: a pit of fire and smoke; and at its heart was a gate to another realm.

Chains of steel and pewter and stone bound it together. Cracks webbed across the surface of the Gate, spreading between runes that I could not comprehend the meaning of. The runes glowed and twisted and swirled, and I perceived that they were the seals which were laid upon the Gate.

Out from the cracks seeped a dark mist. It curled up like smoke, then slithered into the earth. This was the darkness that tainted the Council: the darkness of the Book of Souls.

"Behind this, Chaos slumbers," said the elder, Tai. Gesturing to the stars above, he said, "Behold, the Archer stands poised in the heavens, and the daemon have read the sign. And now they shall drench the land in blood."

As he spoke, I saw in my mind's eye ten men brought into the council room and made to kneel before the emperor. And as I watched, the emperor rose, encased by the dark fog, his eyes wholly black. The men cowered before him as the Council urged them to renounce their worship of the elder, Suri Onash. But try as the council members might, the men would not forsake their god.

As I witnessed this, I remembered the vision of things past, of how Suri Onash was the Great Owl whose people saw the truth of a thing; and I perceived that these men would not yield, for they saw the emperor in truth as I did, and they knew the man they had served was no more.

When the Council perceived that the men would not renounce their god, they brought unto the emperor a sword. Its hilt was in the form of a golden dragon with rubies set in its eyes, whose wings spread wide to form the guard; and its blade swirled like the waves of the sea.

Taking the sword, the emperor asked the men once more to denounce their god and serve the false god, but they would not. So the emperor struck them down, each with one blow.

As I watched, their blood spilled on the council room floor, and as it did, I saw the essence within it seep into the land, guided by the darkness swirling within it all the way back to the Gate. And the Gate shuddered and rattled its chains as it struggled against its binds; for the one that dwelt within it was imbued with strength from the essence of the fallen.

And I perceived that this was the thing that caused the stirring in the heavens and the darkness was that which slithered in the earth.

Then said the elder, Tai, "There are those who seek to free Chaos and see him reign supreme. They do not know that where Chaos goes, destruction follows. Now, therefore, take up the sword against they which seek to destroy this world; for there must be a warrior called out from among his brethren and chosen to lead them to victory."

Then the elder offered me his great sword and said, "Take up the sword, Schandrof, for I have chosen you to be my warrior in this age."

My heart was filled with trepidation at his words, for I was no warrior. How could I defeat an army led by Chaos himself? Knowing my limitations, I retreated a step and said, "What makes me the chosen one? Why should this burden now be placed upon my shoulders? What wicked thing have I done to deserve this?"

But the elder remained silent, his hand still outstretched, offering me his great sword, Azarael. And they that stood with him watched on with sombre expressions, for they perceived that I would not take up the sword.

It dawned on me then that the consequences for refusing such a great commission from the Father of the Night would be grave indeed.

I fell to my knees once more, and despite my promise, I besought the goddess to take me away from this place and end the vision, for it was a great vision that I could not endure.

I felt her hand rest gently upon my shoulder, and when I looked up into her eyes, they were filled with sadness.

Then spake I unto her, saying, "This burden is heavy and the elder lays a great responsibility at my feet; for I am not a man of war or great strength, and there is no guarantee that I shall be victorious, should I choose to stand against the emperor."

"Many paths lay ahead of us," said she, "but all lead to one of two ends. It is a flowing future, Schandrof. I cannot promise victory over the emperor; I can only assure you that, in doing nothing, you seal the fate of this world."

"Then show me this flowing future," said I; "that I might perceive the things which are yet to come."

To this, she said, "I shall now show you the things which will be, should you decide not to take up the sword."

At her words, I was swept up by a great wind, and I found myself atop that great oak tree which was the heart of the girl with golden eyes who had given her body for the river to flow and whose soul had restored the youth of the man who would never die.

PART THREE
A FLOWING FUTURE

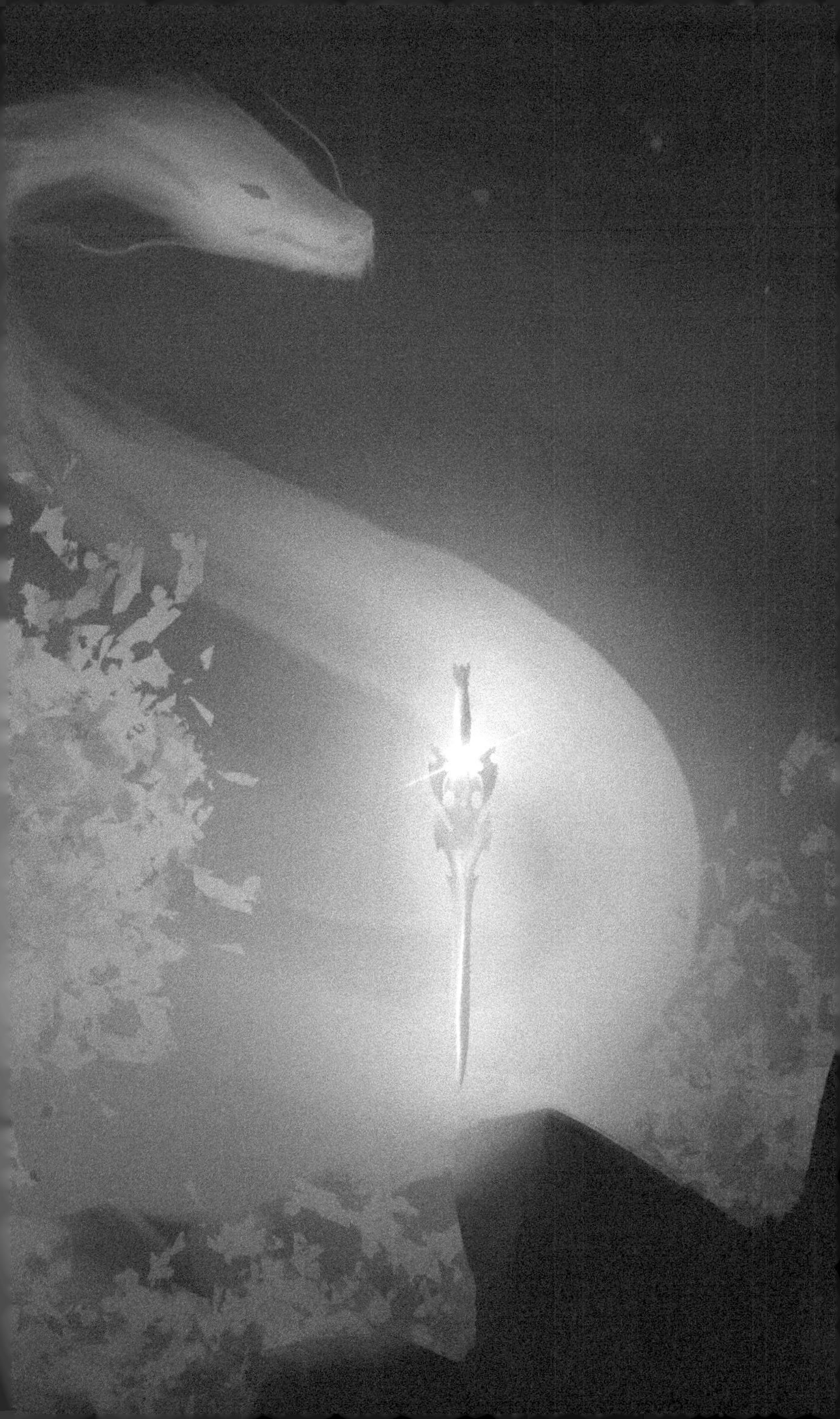

THE EIGHTH VISION

From the top of the great oak tree, I looked out over the land and saw the emperor, Vladicsar, clad in armour and riding on a stallion made from shadows and darkness. He too was wreathed in shadows and clothed in darkness. And in his eyes burned the flames of Sor-Azarael.

Behind him came an army of beasts and men, of warriors and daemon, all seduced by the darkness which hung over them like a fog. It filled their lungs and tainted their souls and spurred them on to war.

The ground trembled as they marched, and the land wept, for Chaos walked upon it once more. And I perceived that it was not the kind and thoughtful emperor that led this army of monsters, but the Chief Arkon himself, for the darkness had stripped the soul from our beloved emperor and freed his body to become a home for the fell beast once called Melzak.

The beast raised his great sword, and I recognised the sword to be Azarael, the one that the Fallen God had offered me—the one I refused to take up. And I perceived that, because of my cowardice, the Fallen God had been slain by this creature of terror and night.

I fell to my knees and wept. Turning to the nameless man with sun-kissed skin and silver hair and piercing blue eyes, I said, "If the Warrior God truly has fallen, then there is no hope for our world."

It was with a grave voice that the man with sun-kissed skin and silver hair and piercing blue eyes replied, saying, "Yea, there is truly no hope for this world; for Chaos is the destroyer of worlds, the one who set the cosmos ablaze and turned Light to Darkness. He was among the three who stood before the Creator long before time began. He it was who consumed Wrath and chased the Watcher throughout the realms."

Then the man with sun-kissed skin and silver hair and piercing blue eyes pointed to the heavens, and I saw the elder, Mi-Kalia, descend to the land. Wrapped in humble garments, she knelt before the river which the girl with golden eyes gave her body to in order that it may flow; and from her robe she withdrew a vial and filled it with water from the river.

She rose and set her face towards the oak tree, and I saw that there was great sadness in her eyes. As she approached, I rose to greet her, for I realised that she could see me.

"This is what becomes of a world none will fight for," said she. "As long as there is one who stands against the darkness, there is hope. But none stood; and now, our world has fallen."

I perceived that there was no malice in her words, for she understood that the charge which had been set before me was a grave and fearful one. Still, my heart was pierced with guilt and grief, for it was I who the elder, Tai, had offered his great sword, and this was the vision of the things to come if I were to reject it. I bowed my head in shame as the sorrow within my heart returned the tears to my eyes.

Then the Great Mother turned to the man with sun-kissed skin and silver hair and piercing blue eyes and said, "I require your seed: it is imperative that this great oak endure; for it is the heart of this soul which has come from within the river, and to a body it must return, that perchance one who existed from the foundation of this world may someday rebuild it."

The man with sun-kissed skin and silver hair and piercing blue eyes reached a hand into his chest and withdrew from it an acorn. And he handed this to the elder, saying, "I vowed a vow to remain with my friend; for she gave her body to the river that I might live. Now, therefore, take back the life which she gave me, that she might once again live." Then that nameless and timeless and faceless man with sun-kissed skin and silver hair and piercing blue eyes shuddered and fell, and breathed his last.

And I wept for the man who had once dwelt upon the oak tree, for he too was no more.

So the elder, Mi-Kalia, took the acorn and ascended into the heavens with me at her side. And as we reached her star, we were greeted by the one with hair as gold and eyes as red as blood who I had seen with the elder, Tai. He hurried us into her palace and to Mi-Kalia's chamber and to the bed where one lay dying from a gash across his chest and many cuts marring his body. A crown of stars rested on his brow, and on his ear hung the moon; he too had been there when the Father of the Night had commissioned me. And he smiled when they approached and encouraged them to take heart.

My heart was torn by the sight, and I wept, for I perceived that he had been bruised and beaten by Leviathan, that great beast who now ruled the sea.

Mi-Kalia took the seed and the water and joined them together once more, and they once again became the girl with golden eyes, though she slept like the dead. Then the elder, Mi-Kalia, took the girl, along with the man with golden locks and the dying man upon the cot; and she hid them behind the Gate upon her star. And I wept once more, for I perceived this was the realm's last hope.

Through my tears, I watched Chaos ride across the land, from the west to the east; and as he rode, the flames of Sor-Azarael rose up from the earth and devoured it once more.

Then I saw Leviathan rise from the sea; a creature with the head of a horned serpent and the body of a giant sea dragon. And its eyes burned with fury and its teeth were stained with blood. And all who tried to escape to the sea were slain by its claws and its teeth so that none from the land found deliverance from this destruction. And the land was filled with the screams of the dying and the blood of the fallen and the roaring of a fire whose hunger could not be quenched.

All were slain by Chaos and his army and devoured by the flames of Sor-Azarael, even the great oak tree and the river which the girl with golden eyes gave her body to in order that it may flow.

When Chaos had ridden across the land, and every creature that breathed had been slain by him and his army, the sea dragon came to him and bowed before him. Then Chaos climbed upon the head of the beast and raised his great sword to the heavens.

The beast shot up into the heavens, to the stars upon which the elders and their people dwelt. The elders gathered together and took up arms and stood against Leviathan and Chaos, the great beast. And they fought with vigour, for there was nowhere to retreat to, for the land burned with an eternal flame consuming all, even Chaos' army, and the seas were red with blood.

One by one, those who dwelt among the stars fell by that great sword which had once belonged to that quick and cunning elder, Tai. Both the elders and the people who dwelt among the stars were slain in the heavens: first the elder, Uulshaa, that great and mighty elder of the South-East, and all who dwelt upon his star; for he was slain with a strike across his chest. And though he fell, he fought until his essence departed from his being.

Then fell Suri Onash, the wise and just elder of the North-East, and all who dwelt upon his star; he fought valiantly with a sword and shield, but Leviathan struck him from behind and slew him, for its great fangs pierced his neck and severed his head from his body.

Then fell Yameer, the fierce and noble elder of the West, and all who dwelt upon his star; and his death was a slow and painful one, for he sought to slay the beast, Leviathan. Because of this, Chaos flayed him alive and hung him by his entrails before carving out his heart and feeding him to the beast he had sought to slay.

Josadom, that keen and clever elder of the South, was cut down with a thousand strikes of Tai's great sword; and he and they which dwelt upon his star were slain.

Then stood Duriel, the one who replaced the wicked elder, Carmen, against Chaos and his beast, Leviathan. And Chaos sought to tempt him and turn his heart away as he had done the elder, Carmen's. But Duriel stood against him and would not be swayed, for he was loyal to the elder, Tai, and he loved Mi-Kalia with an endless love, for she had treated him as her own and cared for him more than she had cared for her own son. And when

Chaos saw that he would not be swayed by riches or power or the promise of great exaltation, Chaos struck him down and severed his limbs and fed him to Leviathan; but Duriel's head, he took with him, for he knew Mi-Kalia loved Duriel like a son.

And when Chaos found Mi-Kalia, she stood before the Gate with a great sword on her hip and a bow in her hand, its arrow aimed at his chest. Then Chaos raised Duriel's head high and said, "O Elder of the Northern Crown, goddess of the moon and stars, I have brought you the head of the one you cherished and the great sword of the one you loved. I know you are a woman of strength and wisdom. Now, therefore, bow before me and serve me as my general in my new army; and I will give you fifty-fold what you have lost today. And when I slay the Lord of the Afters[1], I shall return to you the souls of the ones you cherish the most."

But Mi-Kalia, that kind and compassionate elder of the North, spake unto him, saying, "You are a fool if you believe me so easily swayed—so easily deceived. Is it not by your hand that both my love and my Duriel have fallen? Did each not defy you even as their souls slipped from their bodies? I will never serve you, lest they curse me in the afterlife."

"Then you, too, will die like the rest of them," said Chaos.

So, he and Mi-Kalia warred in the heavens, and she fought with a fierceness that matched the great Chaos himself. And I perceived that she fought with all her strength to defend the Gate for the sake of the ones she had hid behind it, but Chaos perceived it not.

---

[1]. Also known as the Watcher, the Winged One and the Prince of Darkness who once was the Prince of Light.

Though Mi-Kalia fought bravely, she, too, fell, along with all who dwelt upon her star. And when she was no more, Chaos set his eyes upon the Gate, and opened it, and found the ones the elder, Mi-Kalia, had hid behind it, that perchance, they may survive to replenish the earth.

I closed my eyes, unable to watch them fall, unable to watch as the last ray of hope was snuffed out.

The great wind returned me to the Garua, and I felt her hand rest upon my shoulder to comfort me. But my heart smote me to know this was all my doing; for this was the future to come if I did not take up the sword and stand against the darkness, or if I failed to defeat the evil emperor.

And she said, "Behold, the vision is of a flowing future; one that is not yet written. There are many paths to this end, and it need not be in your time, for there needs be a hero in each age until the time appointed for the Watcher to rise and war against Chaos once more. In this age, the Father of the Night has chosen you."

Then said I to the goddess, "You speak as though this vision may yet come to pass should I still take up the sword and win."

"Yea," said she. "There shall be an age when the Archer rises for the last time; and a warrior takes up the sword against the daemon to end this cycle of chaos. But that age is not now." Taking my face in her hands she said, "Come, my child. There remains a vision yet unseen: one that may yet come to pass, should you choose to stand against the emperor and the *taint*[2] which poisons the land and win."

To learn that destruction was not the only end stirred hope within my soul. Rising to my feet, I said, "Show me what shall become of the world, should I choose to take up the sword and emerge victorious."

Reaching out a hand, she touched my cheek once more. "I shall now show you the final vision, my child; then you must decide."

The great wind swirled around us both and carried us across the land, to a place far removed from our time: and there, I beheld the final vision; the vision of a flowing future that may yet come to pass.

---

2. Translated from *Kahva*: refers to the darkness from the abyss where Chaos sleeps; including the power and/or the practice of manipulating this power.

THE NINTH VISION

We stood in a great hall, vast with its high ceiling held up by twelve thick pillars equally spaced, six on either side. At the front of the room was a dais, and upon it was a white throne. People gathered behind the pillars till it was full; leaving only the centre and front of the room bare; and all who gathered were filled with excitement and wonder and fear and awe. And I sensed this vision was of a grave and auspicious moment to come.

The doors swung open and I turned to witness a man enter into the great hall. All bowed before him with fear and trembling, and some wept silently as he made his way to the dais.

A crown of black diamond rested on his head; a simple band, its surface leafed with gold veins. He sat poised on his throne, with a tempest in his heart and madness in his eyes and thunder in his will and magic in his veins.

To his left was one who had mastered all magic, and at his right stood one ready to defend. And I perceived that they both had dedicated their lives to protect and serve the one who sat on the throne, for he was the true heir[1] and the rightful ruler of all the known world.

And all who saw him marvelled at his greatness, for none so great had come before him. And many travelled across the lands to pay homage to this ruler, and all who lived under his reign knew peace.

Yet, the more I beheld him, the more I perceived that this great ruler was but a child, not half a score moons older[2] than I was when I first sought the goddess in the Field of Kesindrath. Then said I to the goddess, "How can one so young hope to lead such a great people?" For the people of the land were indeed great.

"Behold," said the goddess.

And I beheld as the ruler raised his eyes and stared fixedly before him, and all fell silent with expectation. I watched the ruler and followed his gaze to the door. And there, I saw the seven elders who dwelt among the stars. They stood in the entrance, and neither moved nor spoke.

Then said I to the goddess, "Why do they not enter?"

To this, she replied, "They wait to be welcomed in. None can force their way into a heart. It is for the warrior to embrace the truth of a god's existence and bid them enter."

So, we watched and we waited for a time before, finally, the ruler's eyes grew seeing and he rose from his throne to welcome the elders who dwelt among the stars.

---

1. Many believe that the true heir mentioned refers to a direct descendant of the Great Emperor Vladicsar, while others believe him to be descended from Schandrof

2. About twenty-three years old or younger

"It is a great thing for one to harbour faith in gods which they cannot see," said she who stood beside me. And there was a fondness in her voice that I had never heard before.

The elders who dwelt among the stars all stood before the ruler; and I saw that each came bearing a gift. And I asked, "What is the meaning of this vision? Why do the elders bring him gifts?"

"Hush, child," said she. I fell silent and watched as each presented the young ruler with a gift.

First, the great and mighty elder, Uulshaa, stepped forward and presented him with a box of lacquered redwood. The ruler received it, and opened it, and inside it was a blood ruby the size of a man's fist. And the elder took the stone and placed it upon the ruler's chest, and it entered into the ruler's heart.

Then said the elder, "Receive strength to endure the coming battles. For perilous times await you; yet, shall you prevail."

Then Uulshaa stepped to one side, and the wise and just elder, Suri Onash, came forward and presented the ruler with a box of oak. The ruler received the box, and opened, it. And inside it were two glowing emeralds, as big as the blood ruby. The elder, Suri Onash, took the emeralds and placed them upon the ruler's eyes, one on each eye. The stones flared with light and then sank into the ruler's eyes, just as the ruby had entered his heart.

Then said the elder, "Receive the ability to see through all falsehoods. None shall deceive or beguile you; for you shall know the truth of a thing, though it may be wrapped in lies and deceit."

Suri Onash stepped to one side, beside Uulshaa, so that there was room for the fierce and noble elder, Yameer, to come forward. And the elder, Yameer, bore with him a box of ivory, and he presented it to the ruler.

The ruler received it, and opened it, and inside it was the horn of a unicorn. And the elder took the horn and placed it upon the crown of the ruler's head, and the horn entered into his head.

Then the elder said, "Receive the wisdom and grace to rule as a noble and just leader. May your hand be strong, and your name be great upon the land. For you shall achieve a thing which we have long awaited, and you shall forever be remembered."

Then Yameer stepped to one side, beside Suri Onash, and the three stood together, one beside the other as Josadom, the keen and clever elder, stepped forward to present his gift.

And Josadom brought with him a trunk made from cedar and presented it to the ruler. The ruler received it, and opened it, and within it were coins and jewels and cloths.

"Receive riches and wealth," said the elder, "May you never want for bronze and copper and silver and gold. May you and your lineage forever be companions with wealth, and may riches never leave your household. For it is you who are to save the land and all the riches upon and within it. May wealth pave your way and make your path smooth."

Josadom stepped to the other side of the ruler, so that he and Uulshaa flanked the boy. Then the elder, Duriel, stepped forward and presented the ruler with a flat box made from pine wood.

The ruler took it, and opened it, and within it was a robe of the finest sea green brocade of, stitched with threads of shimmering gold. And Duriel took the robe and draped it around the ruler's shoulders and said, "Receive honour; and while you wear this, all who look upon you will know that you are chosen of the gods. And though you are considered an abhorrence and cursed by many[3], help will always be near when you need it."

When Duriel was done, he took up his place beside the elder, Josadom.

Then the elder, Mi-Kalia, stepped forward with a box made of pure gold. Seeing her, the ruler fell to his knees with tears in his eyes, for she was the Great Mother, and he loved her fiercely.

"Rise, my child," said Mi-Kalia. "It is not you who are honoured by my presence, but I by yours."

So, the ruler rose, and took the gift which Mi-Kalia presented. He opened it, and within it was a crown of stars. And Mi-Kalia took the crown and placed it upon his head; and the stars shone bright on his brow and would not fade.

Then said the elder, "Receive peace, that your mind may be steady and not fall to madness; for your burden is great and your mind nearly broken."

The ruler wept before her, and I perceived that, to him, this was the greatest gift of all. And the Great Mother embraced him and comforted him, and when his sobbing ceased, she, too, took her place beside the elder, Duriel, so that three elders flanked him on each side. And it was seen by all that the gods stood with him.

Finally, the elder, Tai, stepped forward and stood before him. All was silent as the Father of the Night stretched forth a sword, in offering. The ruler stared at it, for that which was given to him was the great sword, Azarael: that mighty blade which had drunk the blood of ten and ten thousand gods in the heavens and cut down Arkon on the land.

---

3. Derived from the Retnestian word for *anathema*.

"It is you who shall make the last stand and bring this cycle of chaos and destruction to a close," said the Father of the Night.

I beheld the fear in the young ruler's eyes, but I could not perceive from his face whether he would take up the sword or damn this world to ruin.

Then the ruler opened his mouth to speak, but I was not permitted to know his choice or see the outcome thereof, for before I could hear his response, a great wind blew and I and the goddess were caught up in it and carried to the Garua, to the place where the elder, Tai, still waited, hand outstretched.

And I perceived it was time for me to decide.

THE CONCLUSION

I have seen a thing of myth, yet it is a thing of truth. It is a future; written in the past, and cannot come to be without it.

It is an ever-flowing future, a changing fate which I must now decide. Though there is no promise of victory in the coming battle, I shall lay down my life for this vision, that peradventure, the young ruler upon the white throne may someday lead this empire into a great and glorious age. I shall end this war and begin a new age, one in which the empire thrives upon the foundation of truth. I shall set safeguards and tenets, religions and rulers; that though the paths be many, they might all lead to a singular end: one which ensures the choice of that young ruler.

And when the time is come, he too shall bring about a new age; and shall put an end to the cycle of chaos. For that is his destiny, as surely as this battle is mine.

Now, I shall take up the sword; for as long as there is one who stands against the darkness, there is hope.

THE TENETS OF VERIT

REGARDING THE GODS

1. Let it be known to all who dwell beneath the moon and stars that Pyxis is their god[1], and she alone shall they worship, for she watches over them as a mother bear does her cubs. So long as they keep her words and live honourably, she too shall be with them and prosper the works of their hands.

2. And this is how they shall worship her: Let each household bring of their increase; a tenth portion shall they bring into her temples in the first and second harvest; and let the bastard and the orphan come unto her, that they might find food and lodging; and let them serve her in her temple as the younger, and she shall protect and provide for them as the elder.

REGARDING OTHERS

On right living:
1. There are signs in the heavens of the things which shall

---

1. All the tenets given by the different elders who dwelt among the stars were combined, distilled, and re-worded to refer to Pyxis as the Great Mother and the only god to be worshipped.

be on the earth, and testimonies on dried bones of the things which have been. There is a reason for everything and an effect to every action. What is unclear now shall be made clear with time. Understanding shall come; you need only listen.

2. There is a balance, and the balance must be kept. Knowledge is precious, and the price thereof would be. To take, one must give in equal measure.

3. Be mindful of all things, for an account will be required of you for all things under your charge.

On settling disputes:
1. When there is a dispute between brethren, let them settle it peaceably among themselves within three suns. If the fourth sun shall rise upon their dispute, then let the matter be taken to one who is higher than both. If such a one cannot settle the dispute within three more suns, then at dawn, let the case be brought before the head of the tribe.

2. If the feuding brethren still cannot come to an agreement before the head of the tribe when the sun goes down, let the matter be taken to the tower—to the priests who serve in the temple of the gods. And if, by the morrow, there is still no peace between the feuding brethren, then let the ones who will not reconcile be burned upon the altar at the rising of the sun, and the gods themselves shall settle the matter in death.

On family:
1. First, there is family. It shall always be so. The elder shall protect and provide for the younger, and the younger shall serve the elder. And by doing so, the family shall be kept whole.

2. When the elder is weaker and the younger stronger, then their roles may be reversed; neither is greater than the other and no task is more highly esteemed. For it is in working together that the family is kept whole.

On marital union:
1. Let none enter into a union for financial gain. It is a vile thing to covet earthly treasures, and the fruit of such union is segregation and a breakdown of the community. Instead, let a man and woman be united in love. Thus, they shall become a family and lay with no other. And let each family be mindful of their sustenance; for children are a blessing and must be treated as such.

2. Therefore, let each family plan out their child bearing according to what their stores can sustain.

3. If one shall go to bed with a lover, let them be bound to them for a moon and two seasons after such a union. This is the contingency. For if a child shall come of such an union, their father shall protect and provide for them, be it in secret or openly.

4. If he fails to do so out of willful neglect, let him be shunned and cast out, for the gods shall smite him from

the heavens and ruin him and his family and all who embrace him; and they shall take away their fortune and grant it to the child, that all might know the Great Mother is the lord of the bastard and the keeper of the orphan.

5. If a woman should fail to observe the contingency and does not know to whom her child belongs, then she and the child shall be brought to the temple until the child is weaned, for the face of a father is often seen in a child after many days.

6. If the time comes for the child to be weaned and the father has not been found, then all the possible fathers shall give a tenth of their increase on top of their usual requirement; and the mother of the child shall be burned upon the altar, for she has failed to observe the contingency given for her sake and the sake of her offspring.

7. But if one among the many men shall take her to be his wife, then both she and the child shall be given his name and be made a family. "I am the lord of the bastard and the keeper of the orphan," sayeth the Great Mother, "and I guard them with great fierceness."

On divorce:

1. If the love wanes and a union deteriorates, let the couple remain together and learn to live with one another in peace and harmony, especially if they have borne children. For the Great Mother tolerates your misconduct.

In the same way, learn to tolerate each other, and settle disputes amicably; for if your dispute shall make an orphan of your offspring, the Great Mother shall not be kind to the disputing parties and only torment shall await them in death.

REGARDING GODLY ABILITIES

1. *Ki* is the soul, and the soul is in everything, and it is everything that is and everything that it is not. *Qudra* is the soul manifest beyond the flesh.

2. The control of *qudra* is conceived by desire and is birthed within the will.

3. The use of *qudra* comes at a price.

4. To wield power without honour is a fallacy, and gain ill-acquired is malfeasance. Those given to such deeds shall be smitten by the hand of the Avenger and fall by his mighty blade.

GLOSSARY

PEOPLE
- **Adrien** /AY-dree-yen/
- **Ahazret** /ah-HAZ-ret/ - The only named giant in the book
- **Bartolome** Telk /bar-TOH-loh-mee/ /TELKH/
- **Brendan** /BREN-dan/
- **Enacia** /ee-NAY-sha/
- **Fiadh** /FEE-ah/
- **Leviathan** /leh-VAH- yee-than/
- **Manon**, General /MAH-non/
- **Melzak** /MEL-zakh/ - Chaos, The Chief Arkon
- **Pyxis**, Goddess /PIK-sis/
- **Schandrof** /SHAN-droff/
- **Vladicsar**, Emperor /VLAD-ih-zar/
- **Yrnanon**, Mother /err-NAH-non/

GROUPS
- **Cursed Ones**, the - The people of the land (the Fallen) who tried to return to the stars and were cursed by the people who dwelt among the stars
- **Daemon** /DEE-mon/ - Those who follow the teachings and doctrines of Carmen as laid out in the Book of Souls
- **Fallen**, the - The people of the sky who descended to the land after the Great Fire
- **Kleris** /KLEH-riss/ - A group of seven priests of the Order of Verit

---

CONSTELLATIONS
- **Archer,** the
- **Draken Meien** /DRAH-ken/ /may-UN/ - The Great Wyrm/Serpent
- **Fusha** /FUU-shah/ - The Fox
- **Okami** /oh-KAH-mee/ - The Wolf
- **Phoenix,** the
- **Sova/Coba** /SOH-vah/ /KOH-bah/ - The Great Owl
- **Tradjehn** /trah-JEHN/ - The Bear

PLACES
- **Bleclif** /BLEH-kliff/
- **Catbury** /KAT-buh-ree/
- **Eutopia** /u-TOE-pee-ah/ - Continent, the known world
- **Fitonby** /FIT-on-bee/
- **Garua** /GAH-ruu-ah/
- **Hinansho** /hee-NAN-shoh/ - The Great City beneath the waves
- **Kesindrath**, Field of /KESS-in-drath/ - Believed to exist on the border between the spirit world and the physical. Many have debated whether this is a physical place or just a concept proposed by Schandrof
- **Penzan** /PEN-zan/
- **Retnesto** /ret-NES-toe/
- **Trjingér** /JIN-dar/ - Meaning: Place of Sorrow. With time, the name of the place morphed from the Dale of Trjingér to Trjingér Dale and, in more recent times is known as the Gingerdale River which is the natural border between the Kingdoms of Sabato and Muriel
- **Wodbuton** /wod-BEW-ton/
- **Zenthurien** /zen-THUU-ree-en/ - The land of the gods

OBJECTS
- **Azarael** /AH-zah-rah-ell/ - The great sword Tai used to slay the people who dwelt among the stars
- **Blue Melonia** /meh-LOH-nee-ah/ - Believed to be a magical wishing flower granted by Pyxis to those she favours
- **Book of Souls**, the - Contains the teachings of Carmen
- **Crown of the North**, the - Brightest star in the sky. Situated in the North, this blue star is believed to be the home of the elder, Mi-Kalia
- **Southern Jewel**, the - Red star in the southern sky. Believed to be the home of the elder, Tai
- **Zodiakh** /ZOH-dee-ak/ - Astrological calendar

CEREMONIES
- **Hoadon** /HOH-ah-don/ - The Feast of the Gods. A 2-week-long festival celebrated over the New Moon and marking the start of summer (Summer Solstice)
- **Lupa Grándiál** /LOO-pah/ /grahn-DEE-ahl/ - Autumnal Equinox: Celebrates the cycle of fertility, with emphasis on planting/seed time. This is also known by many as the festival of lovers, as it is often characterised by expressions of love, ranging from platonic gifts shared between friends and quiet family dinners to wild parties, bonfires, and orgies beneath the stars
- **Terigad** /TEH-ree-gahd/ - Spring Equinox: The time where all take stock of the things they are grateful for in life
- **Yule** /YOOL/ - Winter Solstice: Held on the shortest day of the year. On this day, candles are lit and prayers are raised for the souls of departed loved ones. The prayers are to ward away evil spirits and the light of the burning candle illuminates their path as they journey through the Afters. When the candle goes out, it means they have crossed over into paradise

---

OTHER
- **Adomin** /AD-oh-min/ - The innate ability to determine the truth and see through falsehoods
- **Anathema** /ah-NAH-theh-mah/ - One considered an abhorrence and cursed or despised by many. In time, when the races were separated and magic was regulated by the Kuwaha Council. This came to refer to children born of mixed heritage, as inter racial breeding was against the law and these children were often sentenced to death
- **Honohley** /HOH-noh-lee/ - The Great Wave. Meaning: *Here, we are welcome*. In time it has come to be known as the Sea of Honley, situated south of the continent, beyond the border which is also widely referred to as Siren's Bay due to the myth that the Sea of Honley was (and still is) ruled by Moreto, the Siren Prince
- **Ki** /KEE/ - The soul; life energy
- **Kahva** /KAH-vah/ - Term used in the old world to refer to magic. Noun: Power that cannot be directly linked to the gods. Verb: The practice of harnessing and manipulating kahva. The practitioner of kahva is called a kahva'ska
- **Muradora** /MUU-rah-do-rah/ - A healer schooled in the arts of magic
- **Oragon** /O-rah-gon/ - The Great Wind. Meaning: *The one who lifts us up*. Believed to have been sent by the Winged One
- **Qudra** /KUUD-rah/ - The external manifestation of one's ki which can be used to control or manipulate the elements; Magic
- **Sor-Azarael** /SOR-AH-zah-rah-ell/ - The Great Flame. Meaning: *Destroyer of Many*
- **Vientala** /vee-yen-TAH-lah/ - The language of the gods

THE ELDERS
WHO DWELL AMONG THE STARS

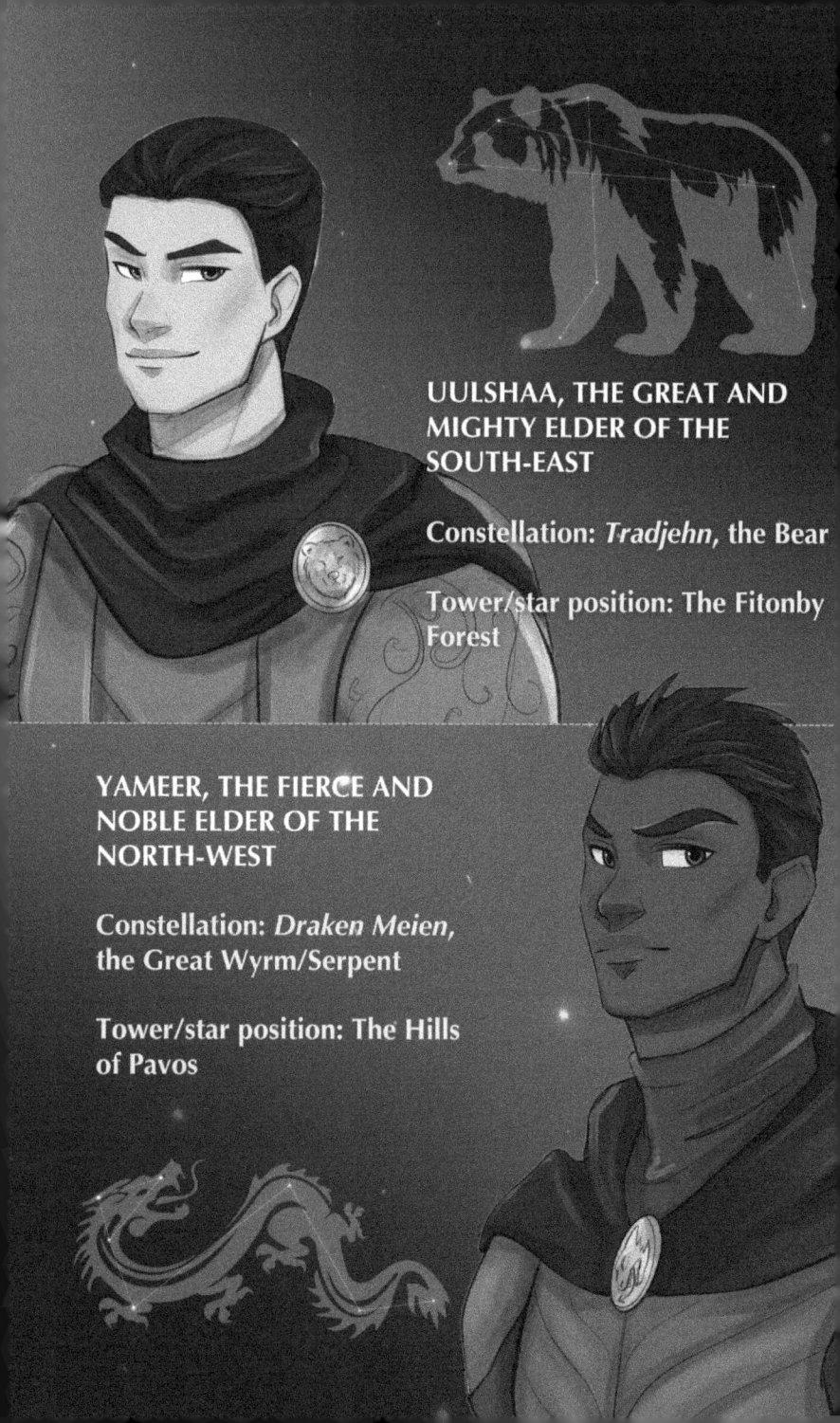

UULSHAA, THE GREAT AND MIGHTY ELDER OF THE SOUTH-EAST

Constellation: *Tradjehn*, the Bear

Tower/star position: The Fitonby Forest

YAMEER, THE FIERCE AND NOBLE ELDER OF THE NORTH-WEST

Constellation: *Draken Meien*, the Great Wyrm/Serpent

Tower/star position: The Hills of Pavos

MI-KALIA, THE KIND AND COMPASSIONATE ELDER OF THE NORTH

Constellation: The Phoenix

Tower/star position: Retnesto

SURI ONASH, THE WISE AND JUST ELDER OF THE NORTH-EAST

Constellation: The Great Owl, *Coba* to those in the North of the mountain and *Sova* to those in the south of the mountain

Tower/star position: The Bleclif Mountains

TAI, THE QUICK AND CUNNING ELDER OF THE SOUTH

Constellation: *Okami*, the Great Hunter, the Wolf)

Tower/star position: Penzan

JOSADOM, THE KEEN AND CLEVER ELDER OF THE SOUTH-WEST

Constellation: *Fusha*, the Fox

Tower/star position: The Shores of Wodbuton

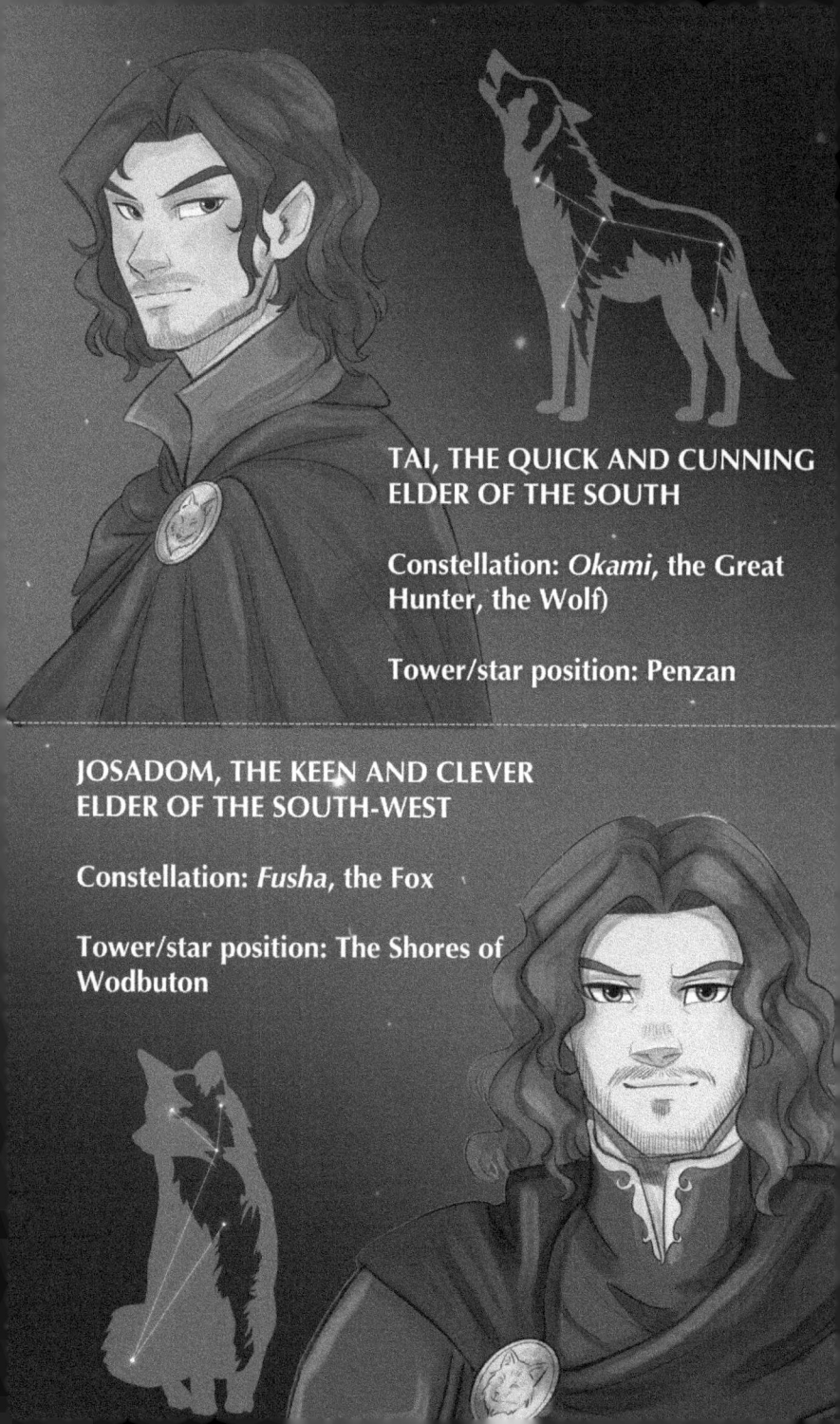

CARMEN, THE WICKED AND JEALOUS ELDER

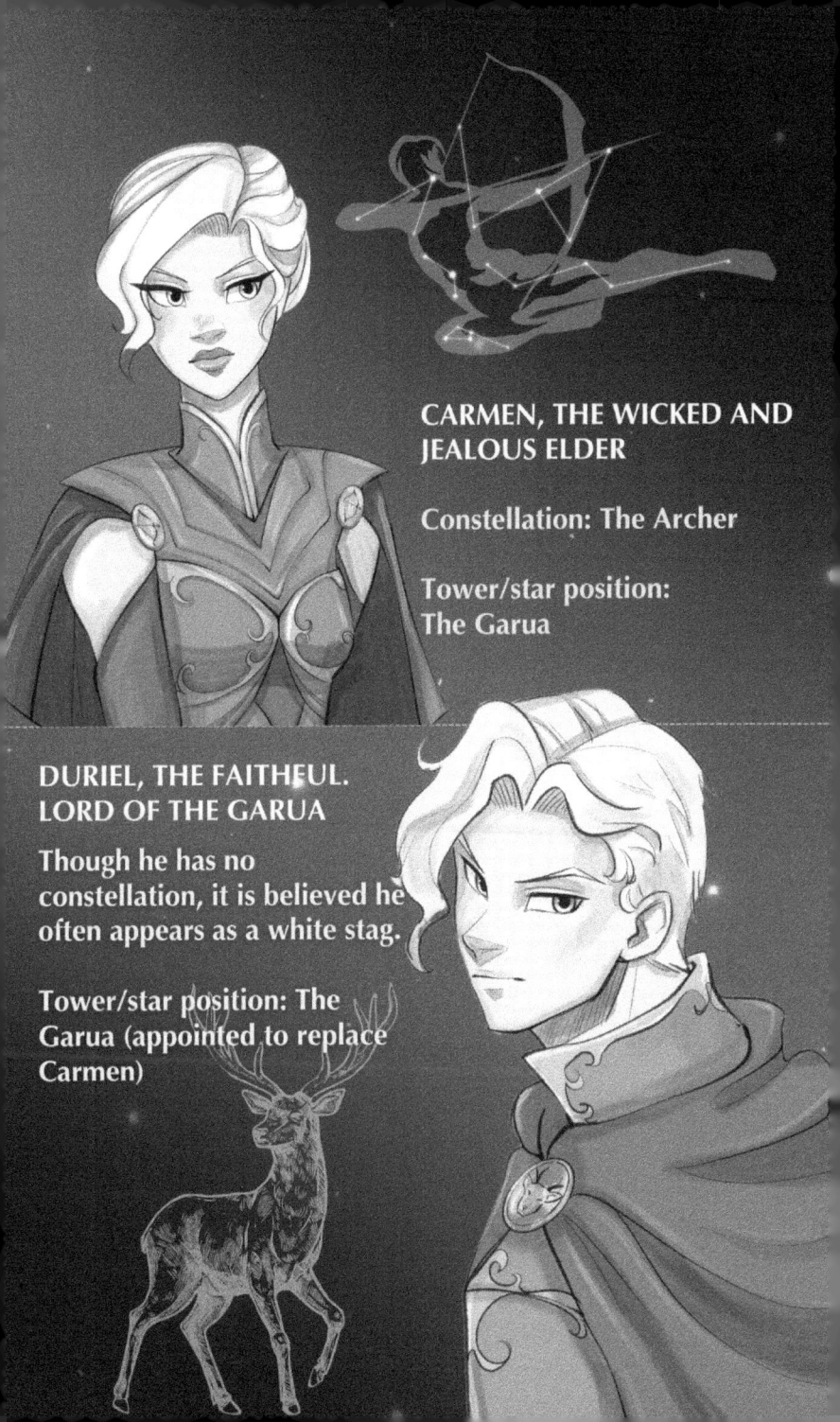

Constellation: The Archer

Tower/star position: The Garua

DURIEL, THE FAITHFUL. LORD OF THE GARUA

Though he has no constellation, it is believed he often appears as a white stag.

Tower/star position: The Garua (appointed to replace Carmen)

THE ELDERS
WHO DWELL BENEATH THE WAVES

LOLA
Leader of the armies of the Eastern Sea

SANTIANO
Keeper of the borders of the Eastern Sea where the waters of the known world meet the ocean

GADRIEL
Ruler of the
Northern Waters

SOFINA
Ruler of the
Northern Waters

MORETO
Prince of the Sea and
Ruler of Hinansho

MORETO'S SIREN BRIDE
The unnamed Yarimaka
who was also known as
the Pearl of the Sea

The Zodiakh

SPR

TERIGAD (EQUINOX)

The time where all take stock of the things they are grateful for in life.

Draken Meien

SECOND PLANTING

SE GR

WINTER

NORTH MURIEL

Fusha

FIRST HARVEST

F GR

HARMATTAN

Held on the shortest day of the year. On this day, candles are lit and prayers are raised for the souls of departed loved ones. The prayers are to ward away evil spirits as light of the burning candle illuminates their path as they journey through the Afters. When the candle goes out, it means they have crossed over into paradise.

YULE (SOLSTICE)

NW

HOADON (SOLSTICE)

The Feast of the Gods. A 2-week-long festival celebrated over the new moon/year and marking the start of summer.

New Moon

SUMMER

SECOND HARVEST — *Sova/Coba*

FIRST PLANTING — *Tradjehn*

LUPA GRÁNDIÁL (EQUINOX)

Celebrates the cycle of fertility, with emphasis on planting/seed time. This is also known by many as the festival of lovers, as it is often characterised by expressions of love, ranging from platonic gifs shared between friends and quiet family dinners to wild parties, bonfires, and orgies beneath the stars.

ACKNOWLEDGEMENTS

This book began as an experimental piece early on in my Creative Writing module. Back then, all I saw was the image of young Sexa playing in a field of blue melonia flowers, a scene which already exists in *Tainted*. I scribbled it down, with no idea where the story was going or what it would become. Within the hour, I had 5,000 words of a new tale worth telling. Not of our beloved little Sexa, but of his ancestor and how he went from a no-name bastard orphan to the greatest emperor Eutopia had ever seen.

I'd like to say it was smooth sailing from then on, that creativity struck like lightning and in a matter of days I was done. But alas, this is not that tale. My voyage was long and arduous, and like any good adventure, was made possible through the kindness and help of many—some of whom, I would like to take a moment to thank.

First, because every good story needs a great villain, I'd like to show my appreciation to James, the man whose efforts to berate the fantasy genre only resulted in us producing great books. Fighting the flames of your blazing tongue set me on this path that has ultimately made me a better writer today, and for that, I am eternally grateful.

To my companions aboard the *October Deadlines*: Rachel, Ekene, Hannah, Ezgi, Tal, Dani and Rahki. I had a blast critiquing with you. Thank you for your input and feedback on my work, and for giving me the chance to read yours. It's a pity our rickety ship sank. Nevertheless, our individual journeys will carry on.

Mama D. and Melody, my housemates and cheerleaders. Thank you for all your encouragement through the laughter and the tears, and for tirelessly listening to me read several variations of the same sentence over and over while you were trying to watch TV. Much love!

Bruna Belfort, my amazing art instructor, thank you for guiding and teaching me in my art journey, and specifically as I created the illustrations for this book. Your feedback and advice is invaluable.

More thanks to Tracey Barski, Rachel C. Hyde, Kaitlyn Deann, Elisabeth Wheatley, Ezgi Gürhan and Priye Okoye who have all worked with me to make this story into what it is today. From critiquing, to proofing, to beta reading, to cover and art feedback, your input has been exceptionally helpful.

Special thanks to Kaitlyn and Elisabeth. Without your advice, prayers and encouragement, I doubt this story would have seen the light of day. You've guided me by the hand and helped me come this far.

Finally, I want to thank God, the one who gives hope to the hopeless; the true author, and the one who showed me that even a little light can drive back the darkness. And as long as there is one who stands against the darkness, there is hope.

Dear Reader,

I hope you enjoyed this book. If you did, I would really appreciate it if you could leave a review on your favourite book retailer's site. Reviews and ratings really help authors reach other readers like you.

To find out more about my books, visit my website at
www.xmokoye.com
or join my free email newsletter at
http://eepurl.com/hUJWKKD

Xyuah

ABOUT THE AUTHOR

Xyvah M. Okoye is an epic fantasy author and believer. When she isn't tinkering with the mechanics of another story, she might be refuelling her magic in a pool, on the beach, or close to some other body of water. And at times like that, with her pointy ears twitching and her button nose buried in a book, if you look close enough, you just might see the shimmering veil around her... The veil between this world, and hers... Between what is, and what possibly could be.
To find out more, visit www.xmokoye.com
Follow her on social media (Instagram, TikTok, Youtube, Threads): @xmokoye

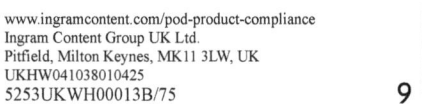